GAMBLING FOR GEORGETOWN

A JAKE LOGAN PRIVATE TUTOR MYSTERY

J.A. JERNAY

PLOTWORKS PUBLISHING

ISBN (electronic): 978-0-9836852-6-5

ISBN (print): 978-1-960936-30-1

INSPIRED BY A TRUE STORY

Jes-u-it-i-cal [jezh-oo-**it**-i-k*uhl*]
- Of or pertaining to Jesuits.
- Using subtle reasoning; crafty; sly; intriguing.

ONE

As I watched the crowd of unemployed actors surround the casting director, I realized that the fire in my belly had become a dying ember.

She was a stylish middle-aged woman wearing an orange pashmina scarf. I was a youngish actor in shirt and jeans, a decade of bit parts under my belt. We were standing on opposite sides of the reception hall of a hotel in Santa Monica, along with two hundred other hopefuls, wannabes, and cast-asides.

I gripped my drink, not really sipping it, trying to look casual. Across the room, the woman in the orange pashmina scarf was being accosted on every side by actors frantic to make a Hollywood connection. I could smell the stench of their desperation.

To my left was a walking piece of sleaze named Brody. All the signs were there—the douchebag knitted cap, slouched shoulders, unshaven cheeks, darting black eyes, expensive phone. He vibrated high, nervous, like an addict, which he probably was.

See, I knew Brody, but he wasn't my friend. We'd

never even exchanged last names. We'd just recognized each other from various auditions. To my knowledge, Brody was a lot of things—drifter, drinker, drugger, dabbler in this, exploiter of that—but mostly a ne'er-do-well. I wouldn't trust the guy with a sack of pencil shavings.

"That woman looks familiar," I said. "She's a casting director. I think we read for her once."

"I don't remember," Brody replied. He was texting.

"I've seen her somewhere before."

"Then go talk to her, bro."

"No way." After nearly a decade of in the acting business, I understood the pointlessness of the social massacre across the room.

This event had been billed as a networking event for actors. Nobody with any power had been stupid enough to attend, except for the woman in the orange pashmina.

"Seriously, bro, get in there, get your face known," Brody said. "Nothing to lose."

"You first."

"Ha," he said, "I don't need to do that crap. The directors come to *me*."

He was boasting, and he was lying. I tried to be gentle. "I heard Sandy dropped you," I said.

Brody deflated. His head plunged into his chest, his lower lip protruding in the most pathetic way possible. "Yeah. Whatever. I don't need that chick."

That was another lie. He'd really needed Sandy. She'd been his agent, and getting dropped was bad news. For bit actors like us, once an agency dropped you, you were tainted, unless you had some traction built up.

"You'll find another," I said. "Keep your chin up."

"It's hard," he said. "I'm thinking of getting out of the

business. Doing something else." Then he smirked. "I heard you started tutoring."

"Yeah," I said. "Mostly high school kids." It'd paid my bills for a while now. Because I'd attended Harvard, word had spread fast, and now most of my business was by referral. I hadn't really thought much about it.

He nodded. "Killer. There's so much else I'm doing."

"Like what?"

A dark grin smudged his face. "Hooking up teenagers with fake IDs."

"Jesus," I said.

"It's high tech now, bro. That magnetic strip—people pay serious cash for that. I got the hookup at the DMV too."

"Don't tell me," I said. "That's a felony."

"It's chill, don't worry." Then he shook his head. "I dunno, bro. I still can't forget acting. It's *stronger* than drugs. Keeps pulling me back." He nodded at the scrum. "Look at them. They feel it too."

The actors had now formed a half-circle around the woman in the orange pashmina scarf. She was backed up against the wall, waving a cocktail in broad circle like a torch against the desperate mob.

I suddenly remembered where I'd seen the woman. I'd auditioned once for her, three years earlier, for a part in an HBO series. She'd cut me off early and thanked me for coming. That had stung, but I had a thick skin. You need it in the entertainment business.

The bad news was that my skin was cracking, in both senses. Corporate consolidations, shrunken production budgets, and creeping age had caused my career to slow down. In fact, it'd been three months since my last audition. That was why I was at this event. I'd rejoined the ranks of the miserable.

"Hey bro," said Brody, "maybe you could hook me up with Lew? Set up a meeting?"

I rolled my eyes. Lew was *my* agent. He was a balding, conniving, sixty-two-year-old narcissist with a heart like a pebble and a taste for girls young enough to be his grand-daughter. If he were a horse, I would've melted him down for glue—but he was the only person in the world who could still set me up for auditions.

"You don't want Lew," I said. "The man's a walking pathology."

"But he'll hook me *up*. That dude's been around forever."

I shrugged. "Be careful of what you wish for."

A sudden commotion caught my ear. The casting director had decided to make a break for the exit. She was headed my way, en route to the door, the crowd following her. I stepped aside and flattened myself against the wall.

As the woman in the orange pashmina swept past, followed by a train of at least thirty people, her eyes lighted upon me. The casting director stopped walking and faced me, her eyes searching my face.

"I remember you," she said.

The mob fell silent. Thirty jealous faces swung towards me.

"I remember you too," I replied.

"The HBO series. You read for the part of Johnny."

"Yeah. You didn't let me finish."

"Of course not, you were too smart. We needed someone authentically stupid. Are you still acting?"

I shrugged. "As much as anybody else here."

She cocked her head, studying me. Then she said, "You should probably try something else."

The woman tossed her orange pashmina scarf around

her neck and strode out of the room. I managed to keep my dignity until the voices of the mob had faded down the hallway. Then I finally doubled over, feeling the pain like a knife in my belly.

"That was *awesome*," said Brody.

"I think I'm going to be sick," I said.

"Are you kidding?" said Brody. "She *remembered* you, bro. That's half the battle."

I exhaled. "She just told me to leave acting, you moron."

He waved it off. "Whatever. She remembered you."

That's when my phone rang. I looked at the display. It was a number that I didn't recognize.

"I always make 'em wait," said Brody.

"We are very different people," I said.

He held out his fist. "I gotta bounce, bro. Let's chill sometime."

I rolled my eyes for the second time. We would never hang out because Brody would never call me. It'd been written in the stars with his type.

I fist bumped him and watched him swagger away. Then I lifted the phone to my ear. "Hello?"

"Is this Jake Logan?" said a woman's voice. She sounded scared.

"Speaking."

"You don't know me, but my name is Joyce. You were referred to me by a friend for your tutoring services. She said you went to Harvard?"

That fact was catnip. Of course, the fact that I'd been kicked out for helping another student during an exam—even though it was one whose father had just died—was never mentioned. I pretended like it hadn't happened, and everybody was happy.

"Yes, I did."

"I was wondering if you had any time available to meet with my son, Michael?"

A smile spread across my face. Her timing couldn't have been better. My ego was a bleeding dog in the middle of the street. "Yes, I do. Can you hold on a minute so I can get to place where we can talk a bit more?"

Phone to ear, I walked out of the reception hall, out of the hotel, leaving the actors' networking event far behind.

TWO

My conversation with Joyce had been short and direct. Her son Michael, a high school junior, needed help with English. She quickly agreed to my hourly rate, and we made plans for me to come over the next afternoon. No more details were offered.

The next day, I prepared for the session.

First, I showered and shaved and picked out a crisp pair of distressed jeans. It always helps to look crisp. Next, I picked out some photocopied materials from my bookshelf, mostly grammar and vocabulary. Lastly, I slipped behind the wheel of my car, and nosed the hood through rush-hour traffic on Wilshire Boulevard.

At a stoplight, I peered out my window. On the sidewalks, office workers were racing out of their office towers, phones pressed to their ears. Free of the shackles for another twelve hours. There were no shackles on my wrists except the ones I'd put there.

It was getting harder and harder to escape the conclusion that acting had been a stupid career choice. If you were a space alien watching a film set, you'd conclude that actors were insane. That's no exaggeration. The successful television and movie stars have simply harnessed that insanity. They've learned to shape it.

Despite my sanity, I'd managed to eke out a living with small parts. The industry lingo for someone like me is "working actor"—which implies that it is some kind of unbelievable triumph merely to land a role. And I'd always taken pride in that.

I couldn't do that anymore.

I looked at the address in my hand, then cranked the wheel and turned onto Michael's street. An unremarkable series of dingbats slide past my windows. That's the word Los Angelenos use to describe a cheap two-story apartment building with a carport underneath the cantilevered first floor. Dingbats were all built in the nineteen-fifties. Today, mostly single people and immigrant families live in them.

I craned my neck to read the parking signs. It was one-hour parking except for those with zone seven parking decals. I didn't have a zone seven parking decal. This was a small problem, because our session was supposed to last two hours. I'd have to go outside and move my car halfway through.

That would be fine. It would give the kid a break. It would be like the way I always make an excuse to go to the bathroom on a first date. It gives the girl a moment to relax, to text her friends, to toss back another apple martini on my credit card. But it'd been a long time since my last date. Women can smell when a man is down, and they'd been steering clear of me like I was a hole in a road.

I parked, stepped out of my car, and locked it. In my left hand was a small bag with some academic materials that I'd had left over from my last student. I'd never really expected to use them again.

I shuffled down the sidewalk, peering at the address on the paper in my hands, then down at the numbers painted on the curbs. Then I realized that I'd forgotten the number. I looked back at the paper, then forgot it again. I was like the dog that walks into a room and walks out again for no reason.

I found my brain and the address, in that order. To my surprise, Michael's apartment was the only structure on the block that wasn't a dingbat. It was a duplex that sagged like an old man in a chair at a public library. Curls of white paint sprouted from the siding like masses of Corinthian acanthus leaves.

I estimated that it had been built in the nineteen-twenties. That was the real golden era of Hollywood. Had I been alive then, I would've joined all the other hopefuls lined up along Gower Avenue, wearing my best cowboy garb, hoping for some background work that day. Back then, the studios had cranked out one Western a week, and they'd needed all the hayseeds and equestrians they could get.

The home squatted at the top of a short but steep driveway. I trucked up the steps and turned onto the front walk.

Three white plastic chairs were parked in the grass. Most people let their outdoor chairs collect dirt, but these were sparkling clean. That told me that Michael's mother was conscientious.

On the porch was a small iron stand. On the tabletop was a collection of small ceramic pots, each holding a tiny cactus, none more than three inches tall. They used almost no water. That told me that Michael's mother was frugal.

I bent over and touched my finger to one of the spines. A drop of blood appeared. I sucked it off and was left with the tangy taste of iron in my mouth. That told me I was a moron.

The front door stood partly ajar. I poked my head inside and realized that it was an entryway. One door stood to my right. A flight of stairs led to a second door at the top of the stairs.

My nose wrinkled. Then I saw why. An empty plastic jug of vinegar with the top sawed off lay behind the door. A small mop was jammed inside. They had just swabbed this entryway. Maybe because I was coming.

Clean. Responsible. Frugal. I was starting to get a sense of this family.

I didn't know which door belonged to Michael—the downstairs or the upstairs. I stepped back onto the porch and studied the entrance again. There were two mail slots, but they'd been painted over years earlier. There were two doorbells, stacked on top of one another. Neither was marked. I tossed a mental coin and pressed the lower button with my finger.

From the lower level of the duplex came a faint sound of a doorbell. It sounded like the sigh of a fat girl who's seen the last piece of cake disappear.

"What is you want?" said a voice from behind the door.

It was a woman's voice. It held the faintest tinge of an accent, maybe Persian. I stepped forward into the entryway. A new phone book hung from the doorknob, sealed inside a plastic sheet. I sensed her standing right behind her door.

Then I looked into the peephole. A single brown eye was watching me. This was paranoid behavior. It wasn't that type of neighborhood.

I waved sweetly at her. "I see you, little girl."

The eye narrowed. "Don't play joke on me. What is you want?"

"My name is Jake. We talked on the phone."

"We don't talk on phone."

She was right, but I've always liked trying to get turtles out of their shells. "I'm looking for Michael," I said.

The eyeball flicked towards the stairs. "That family live upstair. Don't ring my bell, please. It ruin my whole day when someone ring my bell."

"I know, it's terrible."

The eyeball squinted. "Don't bother me. I'm very busy woman. I have many things to do."

"Of course."

The peephole closed. I listened for footsteps walking away, but there weren't any. I sensed her standing behind her own door, just breathing.

She was a fuzzy mouse toy, and I was the cat that had just gotten bored. I turned away and began to climb the stairway. The bright overhead florescent lights assailed my eyeballs. Maybe I was just sensitive to lighting, but this must be a terrible thing to come home to every night.

At the top of the stairs, I rapped on the upstairs door. It was wooden and coffered and seemed original to the house. The brass had flecked off the knob from decades of use.

Footsteps echoed inside, and then the door opened. I found myself looking into the face of my new student.

THREE

If this kid was seventeen years old, then I was an Indian snake charmer.

He had muscles. Not small ones—but *man* muscles, spheres of striated tissue that bulged out from his arms and legs. It gave him the illusion of looking at least five years older than he was.

"You must be Michael," I said. "I'm Jake."

His eyes glanced over my shoulder. I could tell that his mind was somewhere else. "Yeah, hey. Nice to meet you."

He offered a hand. It looked as strong as a staple gun. I warily grasped it. The pressure came so fast that I felt my knees buckle.

"You've got a hell of a grip," I said, gasping.

"Sorry. Come on in."

He dropped my mangled hand. I gingerly stashed it back in my pocket and stepped into his home.

The living room felt like it didn't want to make a fuss. There was a sofa and chair, both covered in plastic. A small television had been squared off alongside a cabinet, inside of which was a set of chintzy blue-and-white china dishes.

They felt very old-fashioned. The last time food had touched those plates, families probably still ate dinner together and *Reefer Madness* was being discussed without irony.

I inhaled. The smell of Lysol lingered in the air. My suspicions were confirmed. This family was middle-class.

It was a revelation. After all, many middle-class families have moved out of California. It started years ago, when ordinary people watched their property taxes begin to steadily rise. It sped up when the aerospace industry collapsed. Today, there are basically only three demographics left in Los Angeles—the wealthy upper class, the poor immigrant underclass, and struggling performers like me.

Michael gestured to the dining room table. "We can work here, I guess."

I pulled out a chair. The back of the chair felt a little sticky. That was from long use. I placed my bag of materials on the floor and sat down.

Michael sat across the corner of the table from me. "Do I need a pencil?"

"Yeah, you'll need something to write with."

He disappeared into his bedroom. I glanced at the tabletop. Once pretty, the mahogany surface had faded with the years. Now, a series of wayward beverages had left an Olympic logo of rings.

Michael came back with a pencil and a deck of cards. He was drinking a frothy white liquid out of a tall glass. It looked like a protein shake.

"Got everything?" I said.

He finished the shake and wiped his mouth. "Okay, I'm ready for this."

"Let's chat first," I said. "Your mother didn't tell me

much about you other than the fact that you need some help in English. What school do you go to?"

"Xavier."

I knew that high school. "The one on Olympic?"

He nodded.

Xavier High School was an all-boys Catholic school. It was large. It was well-known for its athletics, its academics, and its unpopular location in the middle of what had become a Salvadorean slum.

"You like it there?"

He shrugged and reached for the deck of cards. "It's okay. I'm ready to leave."

"How are your grades?"

He began shuffling the cards absentmindedly, the way other people spin their pens over their knuckles. "Pretty good. I have a 3.8."

"Are you taking honors or AP classes?"

He nodded again. "Yeah, a few."

"Do you like English or math better?"

"Math, definitely. I'm in AP Calculus."

"AB or BC?"

"BC. It's rough but I like it."

I made a small *hm* sound of approval. "What makes you like it?"

"My teacher is good."

"What's his name?"

A look of alarm flashed across his face, but it was gone as quickly as it had arrived. I wondered why.

"Father McCauley," he said.

I could tell it would be safe to tease this kid. "A priest?" I said. "Does he make you take communion before class? Do you have to say five Hail Marys if you get a problem wrong?"

Michael shook his head. There was a distant, mysterious condescension in his eyes. "No, he's not like that at all." His hand accented the words with two soft chops to the tabletop. "*At all.*"

"Fair enough. So what are you thinking about for college?"

Michael shifted in his seat. "I don't know. Maybe one of the Jesuit colleges. Georgetown is my number one, but I don't know if I'll get in."

"It's competitive."

"Yeah."

"You have to hope that they might give you some money."

He looked alarmed again. I decided to change the subject. "So what do you do for fun?"

"Work out. But right now I'm too busy to go to the gym."

"Why?"

He looked nervous. "I've just got ... stuff going on."

"Like what?"

"Like, I can't remember what."

"Okay," I said, "maybe you'll remember later."

Michael's hands stopped shuffling. He was looking at me, his nostrils flaring slightly. He was trying to figure out if I was being a smart ass. I had wisely left myself some wiggle room.

"Maybe I will," he replied evenly.

I watched his biceps. "So where do you work out?"

"The Spiral Gym."

"The one on Fairfax?"

"Yeah."

"I belong to Spiral Gym too. But I go to one nearer my house."

He nodded. "Cool."

"So what's your workout routine?"

He shrugged. "I don't really have one."

I feigned outrage. "You mean you don't use a notebook to record weights and reps?"

"No."

"If you want, I can give you some tips," I said. "I've got a lot of experience."

It was true. Working out is an occupational requirement for actors. It's even a tax deduction. I'd been pumping iron twice a week for the last seven years. I would've done so even more often, but there was no point, professionally. I'd never be winning meathead roles.

We stumbled into an awkward silence. It was like quicksand. I grasped at several vines. None of them seemed able to pull me out.

"I guess it's time to get down to work," I said.

"I have a question first," said Michael.

"Go ahead."

"Is tutoring all you do?"

It was better to be honest. "I'm an actor. I haven't had much work lately, though."

He paused, one eyebrow arched. I could see a little hamster spinning on his wheel inside his skull. I wondered what that hamster meant, and where it might lead.

"So you're good at pretending to be other people?" he said.

I shrugged. "I guess so. But if I were better at it, I probably wouldn't be here right now. No offense."

That seemed to satisfy him. As we started the lesson, though, it occurred to me that Michael was like an iceberg. Nine-tenths of him was under the surface, out of sight.

FOUR

I arrived at Michael's home the next evening at six pm.

As I walked along the modest brick path, I saw the curtains flutter in the window of the downstairs unit. The Persian woman. She *was* very busy—if you considered the definition of *busy* to include sitting in your front window and cramming ice cream into your cheeks.

I trucked up the staircase to Michael's door. I rapped loudly and waited for the footsteps.

I didn't hear anything at first. Then I detected the whisper-quiet sound of slippers sliding over.

The door swung open, and Michael's mother stood there. She was a petite woman who looked embarrassed to be alive.

"Joyce?" I said.

"Yes," she said, stepping aside.

I entered her home assertively. She closed the door and stood there with her head bowed.

"It's a pleasure to meet you," I said, holding out my hand.

She looked at it with horror, as though I'd just offered

her one of her son's nudie magazines. She quickly shook it. I could sense that she wanted to apologize for something. She would always want to apologize.

"Thank you for everything you're doing for my son. Michael said that he really likes you."

"I like him too," I said.

It was hard to be so noncommittal. Saying it made me feel like the genial host of a children's television program. But it had slapped a huge smile across Joyce's face that her overwhelming modesty couldn't conceal.

"I'm very sorry I couldn't be here the other day, but I tend to work long hours."

"Where do you work?"

"At Cedars-Sinai. I'm a physician's assistant."

That was a solid job. She wouldn't get rich, but she probably couldn't afford much for college either.

She went down the hall and knocked on Michael's bedroom door. "He's here, honey. Come on. You knew we had six o'clock scheduled."

I sat down at the dining room table. A minute later, Michael stumbled out and collapsed into a chair.

"You look hungover," I said.

"I'm seventeen," he replied.

"That's not an excuse. Were you able to remember what's keeping you so busy?"

He ignored me. "Mom, can I have a shake?"

"Of course, sweetheart," came the reply.

I watched her shuffle into the kitchen and set about the task. She dumped strawberries, banana, and peanut butter into a blender with milk and a powder. I craned my head to see the label. It was creatine.

His mother placed the shake in front of him. She smiled at me. "I'll leave you two alone."

She left the room. I noticed that Michael was holding a deck of cards again.

I pointed at the cards. "You carry those everywhere?"

"It's better than sucking on pen caps."

"What's your favorite card game?"

As Michael looked at me, his face suddenly grew as warm as a November sunrise on the Antarctic ice shelf. "I dunno. I like a lot of them."

This was getting me nowhere. "You mentioned that you were thinking about Georgetown," I said. "Do you think you would fit in there?"

Michael sipped his shake. I could see he was trying to find my angle.

"Maybe," he said.

"It's really preppy there," I explained. "And they're all really smart."

"I'm smart too."

"Not like them," I said, "they're *really* smart. Fast thinkers."

"I'm a fast thinker."

"They're faster."

He scowled. I could tell he was irritated. This conversation was having its intended effect.

"Watch this," he said.

He spread out twenty-one cards, facedown. "Pick one," he said. "Any one."

I drew a card out. The jack of clubs.

"Now put it back."

I obeyed. He then methodically laid out all the cards in three columns of seven each. "Which column is yours in?"

"The middle one."

Michael swept up the cards, one column at a time. Then he laid them out in three more columns, then swept them up. He repeated the process a third time. I started to feel bored.

Then he counted out ten cards. He held up the eleventh one to me. "Is this your card?"

It was the jack of clubs. I was nearly speechless. "How did you do that?"

He lifted his eyebrows conspiratorially but said nothing.

"Okay," I said, "you win. You're smart too."

"I can handle Georgetown," he said.

He probably could. There didn't seem to be anything else to say except to start the lesson.

FIVE

The next afternoon, just as I was starting happy hour, my phone buzzed.

It was five thirty. I was sitting in a folding slingback chair on the roof of my apartment building. I was facing the ocean. It was a good view. On clear days, I can even glimpse little slivers of blue between the antennae, satellite dishes, and patios that dominate the beachfront rooftops.

In my hand was a glass. In that glass was a liquid. In that liquid was a chemical compound that would make me weak at the knees. The liquid was called gin.

The person holding it was called broke.

I'd twisted some lime, added a splash of tonic water, and had walked up the staircase in my shorts and flip-flops to enjoy my big night out, alone with the sunset.

I looked at my phone. The message was from Michael. That was a surprise. We'd exchanged numbers, but I'd assumed he wouldn't want to communicate. After all, I'd goaded him about his intelligence, then forced him to read and analyze archaic poetry. That was for his own good, which made this message highly unexpected.

I read his text: *My friends want to know your workout system. Come to Spiral tonite at 7?*

I scrunched up my nose. Something was fishy. Kids his age didn't openly invite grown men into their reindeer games. They would lose dominance. And establishing dominance was the entire subtext at his age.

Some old thinker once said that the entire cause of mankind's problems can be seen in fact that we can't sit in a room and just *be still*. Yours truly was exhibit A. I was curious.

I texted Michael back. *Sure, see you at 7*. Then I drained my gin-and-tonic and poured myself another. I'd already committed to the happy hour. I needed to see it all the way through.

Besides, I wouldn't really be exercising that night. I'd be playing workout coach, then trying to learn Michael's secret.

And I knew there was one. There had to be.

An hour later, I was stopped on Lincoln Boulevard in rush hour traffic again. There is no avoiding it if you live near the beaches in Los Angeles. Michael's gym was only about ten miles away, but it took me at least forty minutes. This city was a victim of its own success.

I parked in the lot and entered the lobby. A guy in a red polo shirt with the words Spiral Gym stood behind the counter, near the turnstile.

"Hey," I said, "I'm a member at a different Spiral. The one on Sepulveda."

The staffer didn't look up. "That's good for you."

It didn't surprise me. People who work at fitness clubs always seem like they're about five minutes away from going caveman on somebody. It must be the elevated level of testosterone.

"So I guess we're just going to huff at each other until you let me in," I said.

The guardian shook his head. "Soon as I see that green, you get through this gate."

His finger tapped on a laminated card on the counter. I leaned over to read. It said that guests from other Spiral gyms needed to pay a ten-dollar fee to enter.

"I didn't bring my wallet," I lied.

He shrugged. I stood there gathering dust, waiting for something to change.

Nothing did. I swore under my breath and laid out a ten-dollar bill on the counter. His hand swiped the bill, and the turnstile light turned green.

After walking through, I turned around. "You don't want my name?"

He shrugged. Then I noticed that he hadn't gone near the cash register. My ten-dollar bill was nowhere to be seen, either.

"Spend it wisely," I said.

"Have a good workout," came the reply.

I felt violated. I'd just cooperated in my own legalized robbery. I turned on my heel and stalked off.

SIX

I cruised through the health club, the stationary bikes, the treadmills, the Nautilus equipment, the stretching area. It was nearly empty. I started to think that I'd been stood up.

Then I saw the staircase. There was a downstairs too.

As soon as I found my way down the steps, I knew that this was where the meatheads exercised. All the signs were there. The free weights. The mirrors. The animal-like grunts.

Then I spotted Michael at the far end of the room. He was with three friends. They were taking turns spotting one another on a bench press.

Michael shook my hand as I approached. "Hey, these are my friends," he said, nodding to the others. "That's Perry, Chris, and Samuel."

Three teenage boys nodded at me. They weren't as physically developed as Michael, but they were still fairly toned for seventeen-year-olds. The muscles added at least three years to their appearances.

"What's up," I said.

I attempted small talk. "What high school do you guys go to?"

"We all go to Xavier," said Perry. His eyes shifted around.

"You're all friends?"

"Yep."

"You guys bring any notebooks?"

"Yeah," said Michael, "there." He pointed to a plastic bag from a local Rite Aid. I looked inside and found four Steno pads.

"All right," I said, "let's get started."

The four friends exchanged a quick look. I wasn't supposed to see it, but I did.

"Don't you want to change first?" said Michael.

"Not really," I replied. "I'm just coaching you guys."

"But they don't like street clothes in here."

"They'll survive."

"You brought gym clothes, though, right?"

"Yeah."

"You have to change," said Michael, urgently. "The locker room's upstairs. We'll wait."

It wasn't worth arguing about. I'd never been in gym clothes half-soused before, but there was a first time for everything.

I went back up the stairs and found the locker room. It was totally empty—the benches, the showers, the steam room, the sauna. I rented a locker for fifty cents and changed into my workout clothes. They were rattier than a pirate ship's hold, and I don't care who knows it. I don't like dressing up for the gym.

I rejoined the guys downstairs. I ran through their names again. *Perry, Chris, and Samuel.*

Samuel, the good-looking one, was on the military press.

I could see him pushing his stomach out. "Don't arch your back," I said. "Keep your spine flush with the back pad. That's why it's there."

"Thanks," he said.

Perry, the skinniest one, was attempting to clean and jerk. I watched him. He shouldn't have been trying that exercise. He couldn't even get the bar up.

"Stick with the machines," I said.

"But this is what I *want* to do."

"Well, you probably *want* to make out with a supermodel," I observed, "but that's not happening either."

Michael approached me. "So tell us about your workouts."

I'm no personal trainer, but I've been around enough of them to pick up the basics. The four guys crowded around me as I explained the pyramid technique of increasing, then decreasing weights throughout a workout session. I showed them how to use kettlebells, which have been woefully forgotten for the last eighty years. I quizzed them on their diets. All of them admitting to eating processed frozen foods.

"Then you guys may as well go home right now," I said.

"Why?"

"Because good health is seventy-five percent diet."

They patiently listened, but my intuition told me that their attention was elsewhere. They were distracted in the same way as Michael had been as his hands shuffled the playing cards.

After an hour, the guys were exhausted.

"Time to change," said Michael. "Let's hit the locker room."

SEVEN

I followed the group into the men's locker room. The seniors stripped down to nothing and wrapped towels around their waists. I looked away. It was common courtesy.

"We always end a workout with the steam room," said Michael.

That sounded incredibly dumb to me. "Maybe if you want to pass out," I said.

He shook his water bottle. "Nah, we watch out for each other. Aren't you gonna come?"

"No, I have to leave."

"Where?"

"I'm going out," I said. "With friends."

Michael must've detected that lie, because he became more insistent. "No, you have to join us. The steam feels so good."

I looked back at his three friends. They wore curiously detached looks on their faces. Then I looked back at Michael.

"All right," I said.

Steam rooms have never been my favorite places, and

they're a terrible way to end a workout, if you ask me. But I kept my mouth shut as I stripped down to my skivvies. I wasn't getting naked around my student.

A cloud of steam billowed out from the steam room when I pulled the door open. I pushed my way through it. Inside, four shadowy figures were arranged on the tiled steps.

I let the door close behind me. I sat down near the door and leaned forward, my elbows on my knees. I could feel my chest tightening. I regretted those two gin-and-tonics earlier. They were clouding my judgment.

I listened to the guys make small talk about their lives. The rumors about the midterm on Tuesday. The senior who'd just been expelled for drugs. Which AP European History teacher was the hardest.

All of it took me back. I'd been out of high school for more than a decade. The world looked bigger now; adolescence felt smaller. It was like a diorama of adult life.

Samuel was the first to stand up. "That's it for me, fellas." He stumbled to the door and left.

A minute later, Perry followed. Shortly after that, Chris left too.

Soon, Michael and I were alone in the steam room.

"You leaving too?" I said.

"No," he replied, "I could stay here for hours."

I didn't say anything to that. The steam was condensing in my nostrils. My underwear was soaked.

"So I have a question," I said.

"Yeah."

"Why are you guys so committed to weightlifting?"

"Why not?" he said. He lifted a bucket and poured more water on the stones. A few seconds later, the steam had clouded the air again. My student had become a darkened shape in the vapors, a mere suggestion of a person.

"None of you are athletes, right?"

"No," he replied.

"I think there's something you're not telling me."

"Yeah, we don't want to be weaklings."

"That was a dodge."

"Nah," Michael said. "You're just suspicious."

"Then tell me why you're so busy."

He didn't answer. I knew that I was pushing my luck here, that it was jeopardizing my job, but something compelled me.

When his response finally came, it sounded like flesh hitting tile.

I glanced over. Michael had fallen off the step and lay sprawled onto the floor. He appeared to be unconscious. His arm was sticking straight out under his head. His water bottle had fallen out of his hand and rolled across the floor.

I dashed across the floor and knelt next to him and felt for a pulse. It was there. He'd probably just passed out. Common sense said that he needed to leave the steam room, pronto. The problem was that he weighed nearly two hundred pounds. I needed help.

I ran out of the steam room. His three friends were almost finished changing. "Guys, Michael's passed out. Help me drag him out here."

There was a significant pause. I saw them exchange more glances. I was getting tired of that.

"Crap," said Samuel.

He and Chris ran with me back into the steam room. They hooked Michael under his armpits and pulled him out to the benches. He lay on the carpeted floor, his mouth open, his tongue lolling around.

Perry arrived in the locker room. Behind him was the man from the front desk, the one who'd pocketed my money. With him was a security guard.

"What happened?" said the guard.

"My friend Michael passed out in the steam room," I said.

"How?"

"We don't know," said Chris. "He was alone with this guy."

"How old is Michael?" said the guard.

"Seventeen," said Samuel.

"How old are you, sir?" said the guard, turning to me.

"I'm twenty-eight."

His eyebrow lifted. I caught the insinuation. I was crouched, in wet boxer shorts, next to an underage boy who'd passed out naked with me in a steam room.

Then I heard a click. I twisted around. Perry had just taken my picture. He was circling around to get me from a different angle.

"You know," I said, standing up, "I don't like where this is going."

"I bet you don't," said the guard. "Can I see your membership card?"

"No," I said. "I haven't done anything wrong."

"This is a minor."

"True."

His hand came out, palm up. "ID—*now*."

"You can check the registry for my name," I said, knowing full well it wasn't there.

The front desk clerk shifted uncomfortably. I bet he was regretting going off the books now.

"His name is Jake," said Perry.

I whirled on him. "You were in that steam room *with* us."

"No I wasn't."

"Yes, you were."

"Michael said he felt like you had a weird crush on him."

Perry's face was completely blank. My jaw literally dropped open. That was the first time it'd ever done that.

I stood in the middle of the room, five males circled around me, a sixth one unconscious on the floor with a towel around his waist.

This was feeling distinctly like a setup. The purpose was unclear, but it was a setup all the same. And there was only one solution.

Run.

I calmly moved over to my locker, pulled out my flip-flops, and slung my bag of street clothing over my shoulder. Then I walked straight out of the locker room. I was still in my underwear.

The guard and the front desk clerk followed me. I crossed the exercise floor, darted through the Nautilus equipment. Behind me, the guard's keys were jangling as he tried to keep pace with me. I guessed that he was about five steps behind.

Then the keys started jangling faster.

I didn't need to glance back to know that he was running. On the other hand, he didn't know that I was fast. I bolted like a greyhound towards the front turnstiles. It took me about twenty strides, even in flip-flops.

I hopped clear over the gate and shot out the front door.

I hit the street and knew I was safe. Even though they couldn't do anything to me off property, I still ran all the way to my car and peeled off into the night.

EIGHT

I spent most of the next morning in bed, staring at the ceiling. I was trying to decide the best way to decorate my future prison cell.

I hadn't done anything wrong. But the human mind is susceptible to suggestion, and it'd been suggested that I was a homosexual pederast. Half my brain, the self-aware part, knew that it was a horrible lie. Someone was trying to get me.

But the other half of my brain had started to believe the lie. And it wouldn't stop telling me that I was guilty. I desperately wanted to carve that irrational half of my brain out of my skull.

Michael was the answer. He'd know why this had happened. But I'd have to be a lunatic to have another tutoring session with him. He could've been part of the plan. He could've even been the ringleader. Or he could simply be the devil incarnate.

I doubted that, though. Even though he was harboring a lot of secrets, my intuition had told me that he was a decent kid.

But I couldn't just let the situation go. That old thinker had been right. Jake Logan couldn't sit in his room and be still. I wanted to poke my nose into strange corners. Especially when the residents of those dark corners had already tried to bite me in the ankle.

And I knew exactly how to do it.

I showered and dressed, went outside to my car, and began to drive across town again. It wasn't yet noon, so the traffic was still manageable. I kept my foot light on the accelerator. It made me feel like I was sneaking.

I turned onto Michael's street and parked several addresses down. I peered out my window at the sagging duplex. The same white chairs, the same little cacti pots. The driveway was empty too, which meant that his mother was probably out at work.

The time was right.

I stepped out of my car, pulled my baseball cap low over my face just in case, and moved quickly and quietly up the driveway. I walked past the small cacti in the ceramic pots on the iron stand and stepped into the small entryway.

The stairs leading up to Michael's apartment beckoned —but that wasn't where I was going.

I rapped on the downstairs neighbor's door. Then I waited. The new phone book still hung from the doorknob, still sealed inside a plastic sheet. Several Chinese take-out menus flapped out of the margins in the door.

This woman hadn't left her apartment in a week. She was probably a lonely cat lady who peered out of her window all day. That would fit my needs perfectly.

I knocked a second time. The sound of shuffling feet greeted my ears. I heard the peephole swing open. The brown eye bulged out at me.

"What you want," said the woman's voice.

I held up a twenty-dollar bill so she could see it. "I want to talk."

The eye held still as it regarded the bribe. It seemed hesitant. So I rolled the bill and slid it into the peephole.

A pair of red talons quickly appeared. They scratched and clawed, trying to pull the bill out of my hands. I held on tight.

There was a disgusted noise. Then I heard bolts being slid sideways, locks being turned clockwise, and soon I was face to face with the creature.

She was a wildebeest, short and squat. Her tired eyes were smeared in blue eye shadow. A purple corduroy housecoat was swaddled around her fat.

I looked past her into the apartment. Everything had been done decades earlier in a cheap Louis XIV style—gilded chairs, gilded china, gilded lamps. The air held the distinct aroma of moldy cheese. Shredded fabric at the corners of the couch confirmed the cat lady diagnosis.

"What you want," she said again.

"Slow down," I said, "I'm not that kind of guy. I like to get to know my ladies first."

"I'm very busy," she said.

"Absolutely," I lied.

"I have many things to do," she added. Then she looked at me curiously. "What you do for Michael?"

"I help him with English. You want to audit the class?"

She didn't laugh. Then I realized that she probably didn't know the word *audit*.

"So what you want," she said.

That sentence again. She loved saying it. It was her life in a nutshell—suspicion, distrust, bargaining, extortion.

"I need to know where Michael goes at night," I said.

"I don't know where he go," she replied. "But he always wake me up when he come back."

"What time is that?"

She shrugged. "Maybe three." She said it like *tree*. That was a Persian giveaway.

"I need you to tell me when he leaves at night," I said. "Here."

I handed her a small note. On it, I had written down my phone number. I didn't put my name on it. "You call me when he leaves. I'll give you the rest of the money the next time I see you."

"Why you want to know?"

I didn't want to answer that. "Why do you spy on your neighbors?"

She hung her head. "I'm not busy. I have nothing to do."

"I know." I stuffed the twenty-dollar bill into the pocket of her housecoat. "Here's half up front. I'll give you more later."

NINE

That afternoon, I strolled down the strand, watching the models glide past me in their Lycra outfits. The distant crash of waves on the shore, the late-autumn sun on my skin —all of it conspired to toss me onto a small hillock of grass for an impromptu nap.

I woke up with the sun an inch from the horizon, and my phone buzzing in my pocket. I looked at the readout but didn't recognize the number. Many options swept through my mind. It could be my agent calling with news of an exciting audition. Or it could be the prime minister of Turkmenistan. The odds were about the same.

I picked up. Right away I could tell it was her, the Persian neighbor.

"Michael is home," she said.

I stifled a yawn. "Thanks for the update, but I need to know when he *leaves*."

She paused. "He probably go out tonight. He always go out Wednesday. You want I call you tonight?"

He always goes out on Wednesday night. I sat up on the hillock. My mind was working double time. If I waited for her phone call before leaving home, it would be too late. I live thirteen miles from his home. I wouldn't know where he went.

"Sure," I said, "call me tonight when he leaves."

I ended the call, then stood up. I needed to clean my car this afternoon. After all, it was going to be a long night.

AT SIX O'CLOCK THAT EVENING, I parked in a spot at the corner of Michael's street. I stepped out, slid eight quarters into the meter, then sat down behind the wheel again. That would buy me two hours.

This was a stakeout.

I reclined the seat and picked up a sports magazine from the passenger seat. There were three more issues beneath it. I had gotten a free one-month trial subscription but had procrastinated reading because it was heavy on professional football. I had always liked college sports better. They were less mercenary.

As I glanced through the photos of ferocious eyes glaring out from the inside of helmets, it occurred to me that this stakeout could technically be considered stalking. I preferred to rebrand it. I was merely being *persistent*. It was hardly a crime. Most human accomplishments have been produced by people who wouldn't give up.

Of course, I wasn't trying make history. I was just trying to find out where Michael went every night.

Over the next hour and a half, as passing traffic shook my car, I learned all sorts of things about pro football. I learned about salary caps. I learned how the running game was disappearing in favor of the passing game, because long thirty-meter bombs broadcast better on television. I learned that defensive linemen don't get any respect.

Then my phone rang. I quickly dropped the magazine and picked up.

It was the wildebeest. "Okay, Michael leave now."

"Game on," I said. "What kind of car does he drive?"

"I don't know. Is red."

"What's the brand?"

"I don't know. It's red."

"Did he turn towards Wilshire or Santa Monica?"

"I don't know."

This woman was mentally incapable. I modulated my voice and spoke calmly. "Tell me, did he turn left or right out of your driveway?"

"He turn left."

That meant he was coming my way, towards Wilshire. I started the engine. "You've been great," I said.

"You bring more money for me," she said.

"Okay, I will."

"When can I expect the money?"

That was a fairly sophisticated sentence. She'd probably had a lot of practice using it.

"Well," I said, "you can *expect* the rest of the money whenever you want. In fact, if you get it, let me know. This way we'll *both* be surprised."

I hung up. She immediately called back, but I didn't have time for her any more. In my rearview, a red car was turning onto the busy boulevard.

I peered up over my windowsill as the car passed me. As the red paint flashed by, I saw the driver.

It was Michael.

I waited a few seconds, then turned on the engine, flicked on my left-turn signal, hit the accelerator, and pulled into the lane. I was about fifty meters and several cars behind him.

The red car headed eastbound for about twenty minutes, deep into the poorer section just west of downtown Los Angeles. This was the Salvadorean neighborhood. Gang warfare had dropped in recent decades, but in this section it'd grown a little stronger, thanks to La Salvatrucha.

Michael suddenly turned left, off the main road. I followed behind him a few seconds later. At the next block, he made a quick right. I did that too. Now we were in the ghetto. Rundown bungalows slid past my windows. Fourteen-year-olds were gathered on street corners in long white t-shirts and baggy three-quarter-length jeans. The boys looked me in the eyes as I slid by. Maybe they thought I was a wannabe gangbanger, since I'd stayed low in my seat, one arm at the top of the wheel.

They could keep that impression. I wasn't going to stop. This was the type of neighborhood where people disappeared.

The red car suddenly pulled over and stopped. I didn't want to pass Michael, so I quickly pulled over into an open space and cut my lights. I was in front of a fire hydrant. It didn't matter. I wouldn't stay here long.

Michael emerged from his car, shut the door, and crossed the street to a rundown office plaza. The walls were made of beige stucco. It was completely enclosed, like a medieval fort. An iron gate was the only way to gain access.

I watched Michael punch a code into the box by the gate. Then he turned the handle of the iron gate, opened it, and disappeared inside the plaza.

I sat in my car for a minute, trying to think, but my skull had been filled with cement. I didn't have answers. I barely had questions. I felt dumb. Then another car arrived and parked nearby.

From the car emerged Perry and Samuel. Then Chris stepped out of the backseat. He was carrying a tray of eight takeout coffees.

Four kids who'd framed me. Eight coffees. Unless they were doublefisting the caffeinated drinks, that meant there were more people already inside.

I watched the trio approach the gate, punch in the numbers, then disappear into the office complex.

It was nine o'clock on the dot. This meeting had been arranged. I chewed on the inside of my cheek. It was useless to resist my curiosity any longer. I shut off the engine and stepped out of my car.

TEN

I tiptoed up to the iron gate and peered through the bars. The inside of the complex had seen better days. The stucco was peeling off the walls. A dead brown palm tree grew out of a planter choked with weeds. A single yellow globe lamp flickered twice and then blinked out completely.

Most of the offices were dark. It was nine o'clock after all. Still, on the doors, I could make out stencils announcing a medical supply company, a real estate office, and a certified public accountant.

One door, however, was lit up. It was hidden in the darkest corner of the plaza, almost out of sight. There was no stencil on the door.

I drummed my fingers on the gate. My curiosity would not relent. I needed to see what Michael was doing in there.

I looked at the call box. A small sign instructed me to use the pound key to scroll through the businesses. It wouldn't be wise to call, even if I knew the name of Michael's quote-unquote business.

I'd lived in a few apartment complexes with controlled access. Normally these boxes had secret passkeys. It was worth trying. I punched the one key several times and hit the pound key. Nothing happened. Then I punched in the year and hit the pound key. Nothing.

I stepped back and looked at the side of the building. The address was 2703. I went back to the call box and punched the numbers 2703.

A loud buzzer sounded from the box—and the door clicked open.

It was a terrible way for a snoop to announce himself, and I should've left right then and there. But I was on a mission. I yanked open the iron gate and stepped quickly into the plaza.

Almost immediately, the door to the unmarked office opened and a figure stepped out. I pressed myself flush against the wall. It was dark. I couldn't be scoped out if I remained still, at least not easily.

The silhouetted figure stood there, peering into the darkness. I held my breath.

Then the yellow globe lamp flicked twice—and turned on. The plaza was flooded with light.

I was framed against the wall. Like a cockroach in a refrigerator surprised by a human looking for a late-night snack.

It was Michael. He saw me immediately.

"What the—" he said.

"Hey," I said.

His brow creased. "Did you follow me here?"

I peeled myself off the wall. It was better to keep my mouth shut, but cocky might get me out of this.

"Nah," I said, "I was just scouting for office space."

He wasn't buying it. "Stalker."

"Look—"

"Seriously, I can get you *arrested* for this."

"It wouldn't be the first time," I shot back.

He hung his head. "Don't even—"

I pressed him further. "You didn't really faint in the steam room, did you?"

"Dude, just leave. Seriously, you don't want to know about this."

But I wasn't letting him off the hook. "That's why I'm here, Michael. I *don't* know what happened in that locker room. I was trying to help you with English. In return, you try to frame me for homosexual assault."

I made a what-the-hell expression at him. Shrugged shoulders, palms up. He couldn't meet my eyes.

"It's hard to explain."

"What's going on inside the office?"

"I can't tell you."

"Drugs?"

"No."

"Hookers?"

"I wish."

"Weapons?"

He looked puzzled. "What?"

"Just tell me," I said, "or there might have to be a call to your mother."

He smiled at me in a faintly condescending way. I thought I'd pulled out my biggest gun. It was a squirt gun.

Perry, Samuel, and Chris came outside.

"It's Jake," said Michael.

I watched the shock pass across their faces. All four of my conspirators were lined up in a row, and I was standing against the far wall of the plaza. Add a blindfold, and it could've been my execution.

Samuel leaned over to Michael. "Do you want me to get him?"

"Who?"

"The old man."

"No."

The old man. I pretended that the last bit had escaped me, but it hadn't. I wondered who the old man could be. If I'd been paying closer attention, I would've felt the lasso squeezing around my torso, pinning my arms to my side.

Then the silhouette of a figure appeared in the doorway. It was squarish and bulky. Its back was stooped, but its head was held high.

"Who," came the voice in a deep baritone, "the fuck is this guy?"

ELEVEN

I felt everything change. The air felt suddenly tense. Somewhere a dog stopped barking. Miles overhead, satellite transmissions were momentarily disrupted.

The old man walked out into the light of the courtyard. He was wearing a black collared shirt under a thin red sweater with black corduroy pants. His gnarled hand touched the lamppost, but he wasn't leaning on it. Maybe he was just reassuring it.

The boys parted for him like the Red Sea parting for Moses. The old man squinted as he peered at me. It felt like a hatchet hurling across the air and burying itself into my skull.

"This is Jake," said Michael.

"How did he get in here?" said the old man.

"He followed me."

The old man rolled his eyes. "Thank you, genius. I mean how did he get past the gate?"

"I guessed the access code," I said. "It's the same as the address."

"Aren't you clever," said the old man. "Now tell me the why."

I didn't want to spill the beans to this guy, so I decided to lie. "I didn't follow this kid," I said. "I was just looking for an accountant."

"It's September," said the old man. "Taxes aren't due until April."

"I'm trying not to wait until the last minute."

He laughed. "You're a spectacularly bad bullshitter. Now tell me the real reason you followed Michael."

"Maybe you should introduce yourself first," I said.

"Maybe I don't call the police."

"Maybe I don't either."

That stopped him in his tracks. He looked me up and down like a butcher sizing up a new side of beef. "Full of piss and vinegar." He turned to the teenagers behind him. "Is this the one from the health club?"

The one from the health club. More evidence. All signs pointed to a conspiracy.

Michael nodded. The old man turned back to me, a smirk on his face. "You really want to know what we're doing in here?"

"As long as it doesn't involve violence."

The old man narrowed his brow. "This is a place of peace, Jake. This is God's house."

That was unexpected. "Okay," I said.

The old man shooed the boys away. "Go back inside, all of you. Practice twenty minutes of early surrender."

The boys obediently headed inside. A moment later, it was just me and the old man left in the plaza.

He gestured towards the office door. "Red pill or blue pill."

A reference to *The Matrix*. That seemed outdated.

"You like that movie?" I asked.

He shrugged. "It's spiritual."

I walked towards the door. I tried to keep an eye on the old man, but he seemed to fold into the darkness.

I stepped inside. The first thing I saw was the small office to the right. It had a simple desk with matching file cabinet. They looked like they'd been purchased at IKEA. A laptop sat on the desk. I saw a wireless router in the corner.

In the corner, a stack of unopened decks of playing cards lay on the floor. They were still shrink-wrapped.

To the left was a darkened hallway. At the end, a thin rectangle of light shone around the edges of the closed door.

"You can keep walking," said the old man. I turned; he was standing right behind me, a queer smile on his face. "There are no trap doors. No buzz saws either. You'll be fine."

Something in his voice sounded authentic, so I began to move slowly down the darkened hall. I felt my pulse quicken, my hands starting to sweat. There could be anything happening behind that door. Maybe the old man had organized a counterfeiting operation. Maybe he was a billionaire hosting an under-aged homosexual orgy. Maybe my imagination wasn't strong enough to guess.

My breathing quickened. The carpet seemed to grab at me as I approached the door, and I stumbled over my own shoes. Clumsiness was going to kill me if the suspense didn't.

I placed my hand on the doorknob, turned it gently, and opened the door.

TWELVE

I entered a room that was empty except for two circular tables. Around each table sat five teenage boys. At each table, one boy was dealing out the playing cards from a tray, and the other four were receiving the cards. All players had stacks of black, green, white, and red plastic chips, the types you see in casinos.

The boys were playing blackjack. I knew of this game by its other name, twenty-one. This room appeared to be serving as a tiny, unlicensed casino.

Not what I had expected.

I didn't feel uncomfortable. In fact, this wasn't at all like the dangerous illegal casinos I'd seen in films and read about in old *noir* mysteries. There was classical chamber music wafting out of some speakers mounted on the wall. A set of white ceramic dishes had been cleaned and neatly stacked in the corner. A pile of gold linen napkins and sets of silverware lay nearby. Some of the boys were wearing slippers.

I spotted Michael. He was running a finger ran down a laminated document. On the paper was a complicated grid of numbers and letters. His lips were moving silently.

Then he laid down the laminated sheet and thumped the table with his knuckles. The dealer handed him another card. He covered his eyes as the dealer took his chips.

I'd stumbled into a proverbial backroom, home to off-the-books gambling. I thought for a moment that these boys were even running numbers, but that didn't really make sense. That stuff had all migrated online anyways.

"Welcome to my think tank," said the old man. He'd quietly sidled up to me again.

"They're playing blackjack," I said.

"Ah," he replied, "we have a philosopher of the obvious."

"And you're the boss."

"Indeed."

"How long have you been running this place?" I asked.

"Twenty-seven years."

That was nearly as long as I'd been alive. As I watched the boys more closely, I noticed something. Their eyes were darting silently across the tables. Some were moving their lips. Others were acting more casual. But all of them were tracking the cards very, very closely.

"Something's fishy here," I said.

The old man had anticipated my reaction. "So you noticed. They're counting cards."

I wasn't a gambler myself, mostly because I'd never had money to waste, but I'd heard about this technique. It fell in the gray area between legality and cheating. It required discipline, a head for numbers, and a talent for avoiding casino security.

"Jesus," I said.

"Oh, he's here too." The old man pointed to the wall.

I followed his finger. There was a small crucifix hanging

next to the clock. I scratched my head and stared hard. It didn't even remotely fit.

"I gotta know more," I said. "Are you trying to help them get rich?"

He shook his head. "Come down to my office. We'll talk in private."

Suddenly I felt the panic. That invisible lasso was feeling more and more constrictive. "You know," I said, "it's probably better if I just leave now."

"Oh come on. I know you're curious to know the whole story. I'll make it worth your time."

He winked at me, then gestured with his head. I couldn't resist.

As I trailing him into his office, I had the distinct feeling of entering a lion's cage.

THIRTEEN

"Something to drink?" the old man said. "I have wine or scotch."

"Scotch."

He looked at me with cunning eyes. "That's a serious drink."

"I never could tell a joke," I said.

I watched him reach into the drawer of his desk, remove a bottle of Laphroaig, and unscrew the top. He poured a finger into a small glass and handed it to me.

I sipped the heavy liquid and felt my guard lower. God, I was an easy mark. "Nothing for you?"

The old man replaced the bottle but didn't answer. "Have a seat."

I sat down in the chair across from him. Behind the desk, the old man leaned back and laced his hands behind his head. "So, Jake, here's what I know. Apparently you tried to rape one of my boys."

I felt my blood pressure rise. Coming here had been a terrible mistake. "No, I did *not* try to—"

He silenced me with the wave of a hand. It had a strange power. I immediately shut up.

"Then," he continued, "because you're nosy, you waited outside Michael's home tonight. You trailed him across the city to this address. You come sneaking in here like some sort of goddamn cat burglar. And now you're drinking my good Scotch."

I set down my drink. "You poured it. And I didn't sneak anywhere—"

The hand shushed me again. I was starting to hate that hand.

"We'll discuss you a bit more later," he said. "First, tell me what you think is happening in that backroom."

"They're playing blackjack," I replied.

"Tell me more," he said. "Be more specific."

This felt like a classroom. I shifted uncomfortably in my seat. "Well, you're teaching them how to gamble."

"Incorrect," he said. "Only gamblers *gamble*. I'm teaching the boys how to *count*."

His face had lit up with wicked delight. A twitch crooked up the corner of his mouth. It looked like a crocodile trying to smile.

"Really?" I said.

"Really."

This was no revelation. What I hadn't figured out was *why* this old man had a vested interest in doing so, and his relationship to them.

He seemed to guess my thoughts. "I'm their math teacher," he said.

"Really?" I said again.

He nodded. "Hard to believe?"

Yes and no. Instead, I asked the burning question. "Why? Why would you teach them how to count cards?"

The old man looked me squarely in the eye. "Because these kids can't afford college."

That was no surprise. College tuitions had been rising at three times the rate of inflation, to the point where even public universities were getting pricey. The days of affordable higher education seemed to have passed.

Then the pieces began to fall into place. "Ah," I said, "you teach them how to count cards at blackjack. Then they use those winnings to pay for college."

He nodded. "Exactly."

I laughed. "I imagine the IRS might want to know about this."

His eyes leveled with mine. "It's all completely protected. Nobody can touch me." Then he waited a beat. "And you can't touch me either. Not even if I were a seventeen-year-old boy."

My nostrils flared. The old man wouldn't let this alone. "Look, that is *not* what happened—"

"Sure it was," he said. "The boys told me."

I stopped talking. His eyes were dancing merrily behind his thick lenses. I got the sense that he was yanking my chain, that I was the butt of some sick practical joke.

Then I thought of all the hundreds of other things I could be doing right now. Like reading, sleeping, making out with a new girl—and not getting sucked into a shady sting operation that might lead to a ten-year stint at state prison.

"This has been very interesting," I said, setting down the glass, "but it's my bedtime."

"Don't go," he said.

"Why not?"

A look of pain crossed his face. "Because we want you on our team, Jake."

I stopped. That was interesting, but my curiosity was going to destroy me one of these days if I didn't put a lid on it. Besides, I didn't know anything about how card counters operated. He could be setting me up to be a patsy. I could end up testifying in front of a grand jury.

"That's very nice of you," I said, "but I'm just an actor."

He smiled. "That's perfect. We need someone who can play various roles."

"But I don't know how to count cards," I said. "I barely even know how to play blackjack as it is."

He grew frustrated. "You don't *have* to know how to count cards. That's what the kids are for. All *you* have to do is sweep in like a high roller, watch the kids' signs, place a few big bets, and act happy when you scoop up a pile of cash."

I drained the glass and stood up. "Thanks for the Scotch."

"You're leaving?"

"I never should've come here tonight."

He looked disappointed. "So you won't even hear my offer?"

I shook my head. "Don't worry. My lips are sealed. I don't even want to know your name."

I saluted him, then turned and left the office and crossed the plaza and exited the iron door back to the street.

Michael's mystery had finally been explained. Now that I knew what he was doing at night, I was looking forward to leaving it all behind.

FOURTEEN

I decided not to say anything about the card-counting math teacher and his adolescent minions. After all, he was doing a good service. But I didn't trust any of them. We would simply head our separate ways.

I was sure that Michael wouldn't want to see me again. I knew that no casting directors had me in mind for auditions. So, with nothing else in the pipeline, I succumbed to the inevitable.

The Earthen Jug.

I trudged into the unbearably trendy café. I couldn't pronounce half of the ingredients these guys cooked with.

The manager, Jorge, waved at me. He provided me with a day or two of work whenever I needed it. We'd had this arrangement for a few years now, ever since a visiting tourist from the Netherlands had recognized me from a television program seven years earlier. She'd told Jorge that an honest-to-God movie star was working for him. It wasn't even remotely true, but it'd raised my stock there, and now I could come and go as I pleased.

So there I was, the day after my snoop—pouring waters, clearing plates, faking smiles.

It was two-thirty. I'd worked for almost five hours and was in dire need of a break. I trudged into a remote corner of the kitchen, sat down on an upside bucket next to a bag of quinoa, and buried my head in my hands. I didn't know where my life was going.

"Jake," said a voice.

I looked up. It was Jorge, the manager. "What?"

"You all right, man?"

"I'll live."

He looked concerned. "There's someone outside on nine who wants to talk to you."

"On nine?"

"Yeah."

That was weird. I didn't have any regular customers, because I wasn't at the Earthen Jug often enough to earn them.

"Who is it?"

The manager shrugged. "I don't know. Some old guy. He knew your name."

A flash of panic zipped through me. I knew, deep in my guts, that the old man had tracked me down. He'd found me through Michael.

I hung my head between my knees. I looked at the cross-hatched rubber mat below my feet. This place had felt safe. It had been a haven, my own private happy place, where nobody was supposed to find me.

Except the old man.

I reluctantly stood up and exhaled. My eyes traced the ceiling as I swaggered back through the café. At table nine, I finally looked down.

The old man was dressed the same as the previous night

—black shirt, black corduroy pants, thin red sweater. A cup of coffee was steaming in front of him. His nose was buried in the newspaper. I could see it was the obituaries section.

"What are you doing here?" I said.

He didn't look up. "Look who died," he said. "Bill Klingenhofer. He was a real son of a bitch."

"Did you need me for something?"

He glanced up. "I'm not going to hurt you. But I thought you terminated our conversation a little early the other night."

I shrugged. He didn't react either.

"You got a couple minutes?" he said.

"Sure," I said, "but Bill Klingenhofer thought he probably had a couple more minutes too."

He acknowledged the truth with a nod. "Walk with me, Jake."

"Where?"

"Trust me."

With some effort, the old man slid out of the restaurant booth. I saw that he'd brought a black attaché case.

I nodded at the manager, who nodded back, then followed the old man out the door onto Main Street, a thoroughfare cutting north and south through Santa Monica and Venice. It was packed with yoga studios, vegan cupcake shops, clothing boutiques, and happy people. The sun was bright, the air was crisp and cool. It was a classic California winter's day.

On the sidewalk, he turned to me. "We haven't properly introduced ourselves yet, Jake. My name is Patrick McCauley."

Patrick McCauley. That name was as Irish as was humanly possible. It spoke of bar fights, drunken bloviating, and recursive modern literature—and yet he was a math teacher and gambler. I wondered why someone that old hadn't retired yet.

He offered his hand. I looked at it with trepidation.

"Go on," he said. "It's not going to fall off. At least not yet."

I shook the hand. It stayed nicely attached. "Jake Logan."

"Oh, I know," he said. McCauley began to hobble down the sidewalk. He lifted a finger and crooked it at me. I obediently sidled alongside him.

"I don't like beating around the bush," he said.

"Me neither."

"But I do like the way you handled yourself last night. It was a tight spot."

It was a weird comment, and I stared at the old man, stunned. He had personally created that tight spot. Now he was congratulating me on having navigated it.

"Thank you," I said.

"So ... we really want you on our team."

I had seen this coming. "Patrick, I can't."

"Why?"

"I don't know you, I don't like gambling, counting cards sounds illegal—"

He shushed me. It annoyed me that I obeyed. I wish that I could stick it to authority more often, but something in me resists resistance.

"You don't have a choice," he said.

"Of course I do."

"No, you don't," he repeated. His eyes were friendly, though. "Come this way. I have something to show you."

FIFTEEN

He walked two blocks to a small park. It was a public square with a brick fountain, an old Shingle-style museum, and a pleasant stretch of lawn. There were mothers with strollers splayed across benches, chatting, as their toddlers clambered across a small playscape. There was a popular farmers' market here every Sunday morning.

Patrick led me across the park towards a large tree. He stopped in the darkened patch of shade beneath it. It was significantly colder here, out of the sun. I noticed that we were well out of earshot of the mothers.

"This will do," he said. "Are you comfortable?"

"No."

He shrugged. "Last night, I was trying to make you understand something. But you didn't want to understand it. Do you think I was being too subtle?"

I didn't know what the hell he was talking about. The old guy was a mystery wrapped inside an enigma.

"Look," I said, "pretend that I'm a baby seal, and just club me over the head with whatever you're trying to say."

He sighed. "Okay, you need it direct. Fine." He drew a

deep breath. "I know that you, Jake Logan, like to sexually abuse boys."

I clenched my fists, rolled my eyes. That again. I had tried to put this to bed, so to speak, but it kept waking up and following me around. And a formal accusation hadn't even been made. My heart went out for all those wrongly accused men across the world. I was now one of them.

"No, I do *not*," I said through gritted teeth.

Again his eyes danced behind his glasses. This was all a big joke to him. Then his finger poked me in the chest. "Yes, you do. This is why."

He reached into his attaché case and removed a folder and handed it to me. It was a plain yellow mailing envelope, full-sized.

"Open it," he said.

I fumbled with the clasp and reached inside. It felt like glossy photographs. I pulled them out.

They were pictures of me in the weight room. Working out with Michael, pointing to his leg, spotting him on the bench press. Then there were more in the locker room. I was crouched over Michael, my hands on his chest.

"That's just a sampling," he said. "We have security footage too. The manager provided it to me."

I looked up at him. "This is entrapment."

"You call it whatever you want," he said, "but I have four teenage boys willing to testify that you stalked Michael at his gym, then assaulted him inside the steam room."

"That's ludicrous."

"Is it?"

"Yes."

He shrugged. "It doesn't matter. The accusation is just as bad as the crime."

"Apparently."

"Trust me," he said, "I've seen friends go through it."

I hated his demeanor. He was acting so casual, like it was just a friendly bit of blackmail in the public park. Nothing to worry about.

Then the old man clapped me on the shoulder, as though he were a mentor, and I were a trainee. "So, what do you think? Ready to join the team?"

I looked at the mothers on the bench. If they only knew what was transpiring here, in the shadows.

"No," I said. "In fact, I'm going to report you to the authorities."

"They won't believe you. Come on. A lowlife actor who tutors boys off the books?"

"They won't believe you either," I replied. "Look at you —some skeezy old teacher who teaches boys how to gamble?"

His eyes grew very serious. "I'm a part of the LAPD child abuse task force."

I lowered my head. If that was true, he'd won this round of credibility. I could admit that.

"Okay," I replied.

"There's one more thing you should know before we proceed further."

"What?"

The old man reached into his pocket and pulled out a strip of white cardboard, about an inch wide by twelve inches long.

"Do you know what this is?" he asked.

"No."

He unbuttoned his collar, wrapped the thing around his neck, then buttoned the collar down over the cardboard.

My breath caught in my throat. The little square of white cardboard showed at his throat.

It was a Roman collar.

"My name is Patrick McCauley," he said, "but my title is *Father* Patrick McCauley. I'm a Jesuit priest—and, whether you like it or not, you've just been recruited to work on my blackjack team. What do you think about that?"

I couldn't speak. He smiled benignly, then clapped me on the shoulder.

"We'll be in touch shortly."

He turned and left the park. I stood there for several minutes with my dignity pooling around my ankles and a dumbfounded look hanging off my face.

All those Catholic lessons about freewill had been nonsense.

SIXTEEN

I lay awake for a long time that night. Not even three slugs of Scotland's best could stamp out my hyperactive mind. It's not every day that you get blackmailed for an imagined sex crime by a Catholic priest.

There was a lot going on there.

At four o'clock am, I finally dozed off, then woke up a couple hours later with the sunrise. I sat there at my kitchen table, chewing blankly over a bowl of corn flakes. There was nothing else to eat in my apartment.

I decided to go for a long hike that afternoon. I thought it would take my mind off the blackmailing problem.

I drove out to Sunset Boulevard, turned right, then turned left on Los Liones Road. At the top of the road I parked and found my favorite trail. It switchbacked through some dense undergrowth for about a mile before opening into a fire road. That's when I began running. Up and down the gentle rises that were blanketed with green from the recent rains.

It was high noon when I finally got to the overlook, high atop the cliffs. The Pacific Ocean spread out below me like a blue chenille bedspread. To the south, Catalina Island floated like a dream in a bank of clouds.

A cool breeze caressed me. I leaned against the solitary bench and felt the sweat drying against my temples. My eyes scanned the watery pattern below, as if looking for some kind of way out.

There wasn't any.

I was a steer, and Father McCauley had roped me in good. He'd pegged my weakness—that I was an outsider, with no company or organization as a legal buffer between myself and Michael. He'd zeroed straight in on that. He'd probably organized the whole event at the gym too.

And now I was completely at his mercy.

Then my mobile phone rang. I didn't recognize the number, but I picked up anyways.

"Hello," I said.

Sometimes you can sense people through the phone lines. I could sense immediately that it was the double-crossing priest.

"It's Pat McCauley," said the old voice.

I stiffened. "Yeah."

"We need you tonight. I'd like to start walking you through the process."

"I don't really appreciate your methods, Father McCauley."

"I didn't do anything wrong," he said. It was a parody of innocence. "You did all this to yourself. Anyhow, there's no use boohooing now. We're meeting at nine o'clock."

I ended the connection and put my phone away. I looked down. The cliff was mere inches from my toes. It would be a messy end, but at least this crooked priest wouldn't be messing with my self-determination anymore.

I took a step forward. Then my phone rang again. I looked down at the display. It was the same number.

"What?" I said.

"Almost forgot," said the priest. "We're taking dinner orders tonight. Do you have any special dietary restrictions?"

"No."

"Good. I'm thinking a chicken Florentine with twice-baked potatoes and sautéed spinach. Does that sound good?"

I mumbled something positive, and he ended the connection. My heart had softened a little. Maybe this wouldn't turn out so terrible. At the very least, I'd have a full stomach before he socked me in it again.

I turned away from the cliff and walked back down the trail.

SEVENTEEN

The seedy office plaza hadn't changed. The stucco was still peeling. The dead palm tree still stood like an evil spirit. Pulling open the iron gate still felt like entering the underworld.

As I crossed the plaza, Father McCauley stepped out of the office door. His hand was extended. "Bless you for coming, Jake," he said.

"Whatever," I said.

"Hey, I'm trying to be nice. I know this isn't easy for you."

This was ludicrous. It was like a torturer throwing me onto the rack and then asking if I wanted any aspirin. "Let's just get this over with," I said.

"Easy, tiger," he replied. "We're all friends here."

He held the door open for me. I hesitantly entered.

Inside the office, I followed him down the hall into the back room.

The boys were arranged around the back tables again, but instead of playing blackjack, they were eating. The dishes were real ceramic. The utensils were real silverware.

The same classical chamber music was being piped out of speakers. No one was speaking. It felt like dining in a monastery.

"Fellas," said Father McCauley, "we have ourselves a sweeper. This is Jake Logan."

A sweeper. That was to be my role.

"Are you hungry?" he said.

I nodded.

"Please, have a seat." He gestured to the only open chair.

I sat down with five teenage boys. They didn't acknowledge me except with a furtive movement of their eyes.

Michael was directly across the table. He didn't dare to look at me. I felt my anger rising.

"Hey, dickhead," I heard myself say.

He didn't answer. The other boys stiffened with fear.

I kept on. "Got any homework you need help with?"

Michael pushed out his chair and stood up. "I'm finished. May I be excused, Father McCauley?"

The old man came over, put his hands on Michael's shoulders—and forced him back down. "You two have to learn to play nice," he said. "You're teammates now."

Then McCauley served my dish, from the left, like a waiter does. I unwrapped my silverware and put the linen napkin on my lap. This was feeling a lot like a fine restaurant.

It was a good meal. The chicken was nicely cooked, the twice-baked potatoes just creamy enough, and the sautéed spinach bursting with flavor. When I was finished, I wiped my mouth and looked up.

All my tablemates, except Michael, were watching me.

"What?" I said.

"You're the sweeper?" said one.

"Yeah."

"Have you done this before?" said another.

"No."

"Are you a math major?"

"No."

"The last sweeper was an assistant professor of multi-variable calculus."

"Good for him."

"Do you know probability theory?"

"No."

"Do you know basic strategy?"

"No."

The boys were trying to be polite, but I could tell that they were skeptical of my presence.

MacCauley came over and removed my plate, from the right. "Anything else?" he said. "Coffee? Tea?"

"No thank you," I said.

"Everybody up," said MacCauley. "You know the drill."

Like a well-tuned motor, the boys stood up, took their plates, and carried them to a rack in the corner. They'd been very well trained. MacCauley took me by the elbow. "I have something for you."

That sounded like trouble. "More pictures? Of what? Me buying an extra bag of cookies?"

"No, something better."

He led me back to his office. Another envelope was lying on his table. He handed it to me. "Open it."

I was getting tired of these dirty games. Anything could be inside—thumbtacks, anthrax spores, classified documents about the JFK assassination. But I opened it anyways and slid the contents onto the desk.

Inside were ten small photos of each of the ten boys. With each photo was a passel of information—address, gender, height, weight, hair color, eye color, date of birth, driver's license number.

"What is this?" I said.

"I need fake IDs," said the priest. "Just in case they get carded. It's happened before."

I had to think about that. Casinos had a minimum age limit of eighteen. Most high school seniors weren't yet that old at the beginning of the school year.

"Oh."

"They're all seventeen. I need them to be twenty-one."

I slid the materials back into the envelope. "I don't know what you expect me to do about it."

"You're an actor."

"So?"

"You must know people."

That was a flawed assumption. All my so-called people had drifted off into other occupations, other cities, other lives. I'd been rolling solo for a while now.

I handed the envelope back to him. "I can't really help you."

"You don't have a choice."

I looked at the priest. His eyes had grown steely, purposeful. I understood the subtext this time.

"Okay," I said, "I'll see what I can do."

EIGHTEEN

I only know one person who could get fake IDs. Brody. He had his dirty fingers stuck into pies all over Los Angeles.

I texted him quickly that I needed a favor. He texted me back immediately. I dialed his number.

"I never answer my phone," he said. "You're lucky I picked up."

I was lucky: that was debatable. "I need some fake IDs," I said.

He made a small *hm* sound. "That's going to be expensive. Do you know what it costs to code a magnetic stripe?"

I consulted the sheet that McCauley had provided. "We don't need the magnetic stripe. Just enough to flash inside a wallet."

"Oh," he replied, "that's easier. I can get that pretty quick. But I need something from you."

"I'll pay you whatever you want."

"More than just money."

"What do you mean?"

"I want you to hook me up with Lew."

My fingers pinched the bridge of my nose. My eyes squeezed shut. He was really putting the screws to me.

"Listen," I said, "Lew takes female clients for very specific reasons. Some of them give him a ride on his couch. Others are just so good-looking he figures they'll get work with no effort. For us guys, I don't know how he decides. The only thing I do know for sure is that he doesn't give a rat's ass about me, or anybody I might recommend."

"Set up a meeting," said Brody. "I know you can do it."

"It doesn't work like that."

"When I get the meeting, you get the IDs."

He ended the call. I stared at the phone in my hands. I'd never been blackmailed twice in forty-eight hours. It was amazing that anything got done above the table in Los Angeles.

He needed to meet Lew, but my agent wouldn't want to meet him. I needed to reconcile these two motives.

Then I had an idea.

THE NAIL SALON lay inside an obscure strip mall just south of Venice Blvd. near National. I knew why Lew chose this one.

His deepest secret, one that I'd learned from his assistant years earlier, was that he enjoyed mani-pedis every Thursday. He would never cop to the practice. That's why he went to this out-of-the-way salon, far from the typical neighborhoods of Beverly Hills, where he might be spotted by studio types.

I entered and saw my suspect. Lew was in one of the chairs, his eyes closed, his mouth hanging open. An Asian woman in a plastic hairnet hunched over his feet with giving him a massage. Another one was at his side, filing his fingernails.

"Can I help you?" said a woman's voice. It came from a woman behind one of the nail stations.

"Pedicure," I said.

I took the chair beside Lew and stripped off my shoes and socks. Gingerly I dipped a toe into the footbath. It was warm. I plunged my feet all the way inside.

The woman behind the table came around and crouched down before me. She cut my toenails with a small pair of clippers, then pushed my cuticles back. Next she began to pumice the skin.

It was time to wake up my slumbering agent. "Lew," I said.

No response. I said his name more loudly.

This time, he sputtered awake. His narrow, groggy eyes swung towards me. I watched him slowly figure me out.

"What the hell?" he said.

"Good morning, sunshine."

Lew looked me up and down, from the crown of my head to the woman feverishly working my toes.

"Why, hey there, guy," he said.

Guy. He never remembered my name. "It's Jake Logan," I said. "I'm one of your clients, remember?"

"Of course, Jake," he said. "Sure, I remember you, sure." He glanced guiltily at his feet. "Well, now you know my big secret."

"No judgments," I said. "It's manly, right?"

"I gotta keep 'em soft and pretty for the ladies," he said. Then he cast a sharp eye at me. "You just wandered in here by accident?"

I shook my head. "You wish."

"So you need something?"

"I need you to take a meeting with someone."

He wiped the frustration off his face and began talking to himself. "This kid. The balls on him." Then he looked at me and answered with as close to a professional tone in his voice as he could muster. "I'm sorry, but I'm not accepting new clients at this time, Jake."

"I didn't ask you to do that. I just asked you to take a meeting."

"No."

"You have to."

I delivered the news in a matter-of-fact way. He didn't like the sound of that. His eyes narrowed. "What've you got?"

"This."

I settled back and outlined for him what was happening. The tutoring gig with Michael, the setup in the health club, the card-counting teenagers, the blackmailing priest, the request for fake IDs, and the actor who could supply them.

"And all this guy wants is a meeting with you," I finished.

He pursed his lips. "That's a good story," he said. "Write that one down and you could sell it."

"It's not a joke."

Lew started to get out of his chair. "You oughta lay off the mushrooms. Go to church, or whatever you *goyim* do to stop hallucinating."

I stood up and grabbed his arm. "Listen, if you don't help, it's going to be a bad ending. I could be denounced as a gay pedophile on the evening news."

I was standing ankle deep in the water around the base of pedicure chair. Lew was posed the same in his. We looked like a pair of rice paddy farmers.

"Tough rocks for you," he said.

It was time for the heavy artillery. "Lew, you're my representative."

"So?"

"Your agency represents children too."

I left the rest unspoken. I watched the awareness dawn in his eyes. His face turned slightly ashen. His jaw opened and closed, like a gasping fish.

"You've got a point, buddy," he said. "That's a damn good point." He pulled out his cell phone and dialed a number. "Brenda, I want you to call a guy named—"

"Brody," I said.

"Brody. Yeah, just Brody. No, the last name doesn't matter. His number is—"

I opened my phone and read the number to him; he repeated it to Brenda. "Set up a meeting this afternoon. I want him in my office ASAP."

Lew ended the call. Then he looked at me with cunning in his eyes. "You're a hell of a negotiator, Jake. Maybe if acting doesn't work out, you could work as my assistant."

"I'd rather scoop out my eyeballs with a rusty spoon," I said.

"Your choice," he replied, shrugging. Lew pulled on his thin black socks over his feet. They were like hosiery. Then he slipped on his tassel loafers.

"So who else knows that I come here?"

"That depends on how quickly I get those fake IDs," I said.

"*Oy*, you're a bulldozer."

"A bulldozer that's still available for auditions," I reminded him. "Maybe I'm ready to play a villain now?"

Lew sneered. "You should be so lucky. I'll call you."

I knew one thing for sure. When Lew, or anyone in

Hollywood, says that he'll call you, rest assured that the phone will never, ever ring.

My agent tossed a bill at the pedicurist and walked out of the salon. He ignored me. I would have ignored me too.

"You want me finish?" said the girl at my feet.

"Absolutely," I said, settling back in the chair. "Give me what Lew got, but make it even better."

NINETEEN

Three days passed, and not a person in the world attempted to contact me. I didn't reach out either. I didn't even leave my house. That's what an accusation can do to your spirits, even a made-up one.

On the third afternoon, there was a knock at the door. It was a UPS man. "Jake Logan?" he said. "Sign here."

I signed and took the package and ripped it open. Ten fake IDs spilled into my hand. Each one had the photo of one of the teenage boys, subtly touched up to look slightly older. Each birth date indicated twenty-one years old. Each card had a fake magnetic strip along the back.

I picked up my phone and dialed McCauley's number. He didn't pick up. He was a teacher at Xavier High School, however. I found the school number quickly online and dialed. When the lady at the switchboard answered, I asked for him by name. She transferred me to a place called the Jesuit Residence.

"Hello," said a man's voice.

"I'm looking for Father Patrick McCauley," I said.

"So am I." It was reedy and petulant, like a scorned wife.

"Doesn't he live here?"

"Supposedly. We never know where he is."

"Can I leave a message?"

"You can try, but he doesn't like to pick up his messages."

"Just tell him that Jake Logan has the stuff he wanted."

There was a pause. "And what kind of *stuff* might that be?"

"The kind that doesn't like questions."

He made an exasperated sound. "You're worse than he is. No promises."

"Then thanks for nothing."

"You too."

We hung up at the same time. I looked at my phone. That message had a better chance of getting through a booby-trapped border tunnel than it did of finding its way to McCauley.

Instead, I pulled up Michael's phone number and texted him: *Tell McCauley they're ready.*

I hit send, then wrapped myself in a bathrobe and stretched back on my couch. That was more than enough activity for one day. Tonight would be a nice date with my books and my imagination. Maybe I could take a crack at one of the nineteenth-century Russian novels gathering dust at the top of my bookshelf. I had the right amount of time, the appropriate soul-emptiness.

Then my phone began to ring. I frowned and picked it. The display said McCauley.

"What?" I said crankily.

"It's been reported to me," said the baritone, "that you have some important items in your possession."

I didn't have the energy or the gumption to mess with my blackmailer, so I just gave it to him straight. "Yeah, I do."

"Bring them to the H.M.S. Bounty at 7 pm tonight."

"Is that a ship?"

"It's a bar on Wilshire. Look it up."

He ended the phone call. I exhaled. This job was ruining my new lifestyle. I would have to shower, shave, look presentable.

That Russian novel was going to have to wait. It was okay. I probably couldn't have kept any of the characters straight anyways.

TWENTY

It was only fifteen miles, but the drive took over an hour and a half because of rush-hour traffic. I didn't know how much worse congestion could get. Then I remembered reading about how, in São Paulo, the rich literally fly in helicopters around the city to avoid traffic.

Apparently, it could get a lot worse.

I was looking for a tall apartment-hotel called the Gaylord. My eyes spotted the swooping green sign from a mile away. As I drew closer, I peered through the windshield in astonishment.

The building was an art deco relic from the nineteen-thirties, the type of place that rented by the month to single men who'd lost their homes and wives. I could picture them, those Depression-era sad sacks, sitting at the edges of their thin mattresses, wearing white undershirts and suspenders with their gray dress pants, their heads in their hands, empty bottles of whiskey at their feet.

If I'd been living in those days, it probably would have been my home too.

It was seven o'clock, and the parking restrictions had just

lifted, so I grabbed one of the curbside spots. They would fill up soon with partiers headed to *soju* hotspots in Koreatown.

I fed the meter, stuffed the folder bearing the fake IDs into my inside coat pocket, and danced between the traffic across Wilshire Boulevard.

The entrance to the bar consisted of a pair of wooden doors. They looked nautical. I pushed through them and found myself inside a totally dark vestibule, facing a second pair of double doors. I pushed through those too.

Finally I found myself in the H.M.S. Bounty. It was decorated with circular red leather booths, brass name-plates, shipyard décor. This room had been here for nearly a century, serving drinks to several generations of actors and failures. But I repeat myself.

On the barstools, under the hanging glassware, hunched a row of eight elderly shoulders. They sagged with the accumulated weight of age, disappointment, and whiskey.

At the far end of the stools sat Father McCauley. He had his nose deep inside a glass of brown liquid.

I didn't want to waste any time. This would be quick. It didn't take long to end blackmail.

I pulled myself up to my full height and approached the old priest. "Special delivery. Are you Father Patrick McCauley?"

The old priest turned around on his stool. There was fear on his face. That was an odd reaction.

He grasped me by the neck and pulled my head in close to his. Then he nodded towards the other men drinking. "These old bastards aren't supposed to know I'm a priest."

"Sorry," I said.

"It's all right, you didn't know." He released me. "Thank God, they can't hear a damn thing."

"Here's your package."

"Okay, let's see it." He donned a pair of glasses.

I handed him the folder. He stuck his hand inside, rustled around, and inspected it. I noticed that he was careful not to bring it out in public.

"This is good work," he said, then closed the folder. He stowed it in his black attaché case that was at his feet. "You know the right people."

"Some would say the wrong people."

"I got a scotch ready for you." He slid a second glass of brown liquid towards me across the countertop. "It's neat. I didn't know when you'd be here."

"I can't really stay," I lied.

"Have a drink, Jake."

He grinned. The subtext sank in. This old priest was still holding the strings above my head, and my little wooden limbs were dancing and jerking, the way they would, now and forevermore.

Frowning, I pulled out the stool. I settled myself upon it like a chicken whose feathers had been severely ruffled. Then I took my first sip of the scotch.

"You like it?" he asked.

"I'm not spitting it across the room."

"Well put."

I looked at his hands, wrapped around the glass. The veins were engorged and green.

He noticed me looking. "The ravages of time," he said. "I'll be seventy-seven years old next week."

"Congratulations."

He laughed at that. I didn't know why. Maybe it was just his type of blowsy Irish humor. Or maybe he was just drunk enough to laugh at anything.

"So what would you like to know about me? This is your one and only chance to ask questions."

"I don't care," I replied. "Just be sure to lift my head off the bar when you come to the good parts."

He laughed again. "I like you, Jake." He signaled the bartender, who quickly came over and poured another scotch.

"Did you know," he began, "that before I was a priest, I was a mathematician?"

I shook my head no.

"It's true. Back in the early sixties. I was a Ph.D. candidate in probability at UCLA. Twenty-three years old. Well, one thing led to another, and I ended up working with Ed Thorpe. He was my teacher."

McCauley looked at me, waiting for that to sink in. But I was a slab of concrete, and it didn't.

"Who's Ed Thorpe?" I said.

"He wrote *Beat the Dealer*."

I shrugged. That meant nothing to me.

"It's the seminal work. The Bible of card-counters." He tapped his own sternum with a finger. "I was his assistant."

"And then you became a priest after that?" I said.

"It's unusual, I know," he said. "Here's what happened. Between 1962 and 1965, counters were cleaning up. I took advantage of the era."

"How?"

"The pit bosses in Vegas were goons, no education whatsoever. They could spot cheats, but they couldn't understand a running count. Face card density flew over their heads. It wasn't until the casinos went corporate that people with M.B.A.s took over. *They* understood math. So they cracked down. And I got expelled from Eden."

"Really?" I said.

"Yep."

I imagined him being tied up and beaten in a back room. The old priest seemed to read my mind. "Nobody ever hurt me. That era of mob violence was over by then anyways. But I was finished, barred, *persona non grata*. I was finished with higher mathematics too—I'd blown that opportunity. And I wanted to atone for my greed. So I joined the Jesuits." He leaned back and spread his palms to the ceiling. "Now I've been in the order for almost fifty years."

I didn't know what to say. His life story was outrageous yet plausible.

"So explain to me one more time," I said, "why you're helping teenage kids count cards at blackjack."

"To pay for college." His eyes were deadly serious. "It's outrageous. Higher education is in an enormous bubble. Nobody can afford college anymore. And God help anyone who wants to go into the liberal arts."

"So you find the poorest kids at your high school—"

"No," he corrected, "the poorest kids qualify for financial aid. I only take the *middle-class* kids. They're the ones getting caught in the gap. They don't have enough savings to pay for college, but they don't get much assistance either."

"It makes sense."

"Sure," he said, "especially since American life teaches us to climb the ladder, away from the losers. Me, I'm going down the ladder. Jesuits have been doing this for five hundred years anyways—founding hospitals, cleaning prisons, reforming prostitutes, organizing resistance to famine and floods. Our saint, Aloysius Gonzaga, died at age twenty-one while helping plague victims."

He suddenly pounded his fist on the table. "These families have a financial plague, Jake. I can help them. It's my moral *duty* to help them."

"By stealing money from casinos," I said.

The old priest grew annoyed. "You're not getting it. Jesus Christ *himself* threw moneychangers out of the temple. My team of pimply seventeen-year-old boys is *legally* winning hundreds of thousands of dollars, year after year, from gambling tables. And they're buying education with it. Tell me what's *immoral* about that."

His finger jabbed the bar counter, his eyes wild with fire. I couldn't disagree. Stealing money from the rich and giving it to the poor was a tale as old as time. This man was Robin Hood in a cleric's collar.

"So do their parents know?" I said.

"Do they know?" said the priest. He was nearly shouting now. "Good Lord, son, they encourage it! They fight for their kids to get on my team." He held up a stern finger. "But I limit the team to ten boys a year. The requirements are simple. They have to be middle class, they have to be good at computation and probability, and they have to be mature. That last one is usually the problem."

I drained the last of my scotch and slapped my hands on the counter. It was the universal sign of time-to-leave.

"It's been real," I said, "but I'm out of here."

"So soon?"

"I do have one more question, Father," I said. "Does this release me from the blackmail? Am I off the hook?"

He grinned like a crocodile that has just allowed a gazelle to walk away from the river unmolested. "No. I will still ruin you in a heartbeat. But I hope you understand that this is a benign dictatorship."

I shrugged. "If you say so."

"Trust me. I'll make everything worth your while."

McCauley reached down into his bag and produced a paperback book. He handed it to me. It was a blackjack manual.

"You don't need to learn how to count cards," he continued, "but you do need to know basic strategy. Study this book and then call Michael. He'll make sure you're up to speed. Then come to me for the final exam."

"I don't want to help Michael anymore."

He shook his head. "You won't, Jake. This time, he'll be helping *you*."

McCauley extended his hand. I reluctantly shook it, then slid off the stool and headed out of the H.M.S. Bounty. On the sidewalk, a strange feeling was growing inside of me.

I hated to admit it, but that feeling was excitement.

TWENTY-ONE

The next morning, I went up to the roof of my apartment. It's where I do all my serious thinking and studying.

I unfolded the canvas chair that I keep stowed up there, behind the chimney, and pointed it facing the ocean. Then I found, ironically, a card table that a previous tenant had forgotten after a late-night rooftop debauch. I plunked that down too and put the blackjack book and a deck of cards on top.

It was a poor man's blackjack table. But it was mine.

I settled down in the chair and gazed out over the rooftops of the beachside community. It was an overcast morning. The marine layer was draped over the neighborhood like a ratty afghan. This didn't look like it was going to burn off. The whole day would be cloaked in gray.

Opening the book, I began to read about card-counting. The phenomenon was based on the idea that if a player kept a running tally of the cards that had already been played—assigning a +1 (9 and higher), -1 (7 and lower), or 0 (an 8) to every card—he could better predict the upcoming cards.

However, the book noted, casinos usually used more than one deck at a table. Even worse, they usually didn't play all the way to bottom of the deck. And the management watched players closely for possible counters.

I scratched my head, glad that I wouldn't be needed for the actual counting. It seemed like an enormous pain.

Instead, I began to concentrate on learning basic strategy. Those principles, I read, had been first cracked back in 1956 by a team of mathematicians headed by Roger Baldwin. This team had found that, under the rules of basic strategy, the casino had a meager .62% advantage.

They had published their findings in the *Journal of the American Statistical Association*. This article had stimulated further research, which was undertaken by organizations as varied as IBM, MIT, Jet Propulsion Laboratory, and even the Atomic Energy Commission.

Those groups came to a better conclusion. When properly played, basic strategy gives a .1% *advantage* to the player.

I put the book down. This floored me. I'd always assumed that every single game favored the house. Blackjack, it seemed, was one that the casino could potentially *lose*—and the only thing keeping that from happening was the ignorance of the average gambler.

Suddenly the cocktail waitresses, the cleavage, the free drinks, and the confusing floor plans made a lot of sense. Get the customers drunk or distracted and confused, and they make mistakes. You save your bottom line on what could be a losing game.

The curtain had been pulled back. I felt a sudden rush of excitement. If I just learned basic strategy, I could help win hundreds of thousands of dollars. It was guaranteed. I wondered what fraction of that McCauley was planning to share with me.

Energized, I dove headlong into basic strategy. I learned the fundamental precepts quickly, then began to memorize the important variations and exceptions. *Double down on any first two cards. Resplit all pairs except aces. Dealer stands on a soft 17. Always hit a stiff when the dealer is showing a strong card—unless holding a (7,7) to the dealer's 10.*

Four hours later, I felt heat on the back of my neck. I looked up, squinting. The gray marine layer had lifted. Sunshine had arrived.

I reached for my phone and texted Michael. He may have the upper hand, but I wasn't going to leave without raking him across the coals.

TWENTY-TWO

Three hours later, I swaggered up to Michael's house. The kid would grovel. I would make him.

The house knelt before me like a monk on his knees. As I stepped into the small foyer, the wildebeest's door opened. She wore the same blue eye shadow, the same purple robe, the same stench of moldy cheese.

"I want the money," she said. "You promise."

"Next time, sweetheart," I replied.

"I need now. I am busy person."

I laughed. "Are you really back to that again?"

I head up the stairs. Even with my back turned, I could sense the wildebeest watching me, spirals of steam curling out of her nostrils.

Michael answered the door before I could even knock. I plunged inside, and he shut the door. "She's messed up," he said.

"Yeah, must be something in the water around here."

He ignored the jab, and I took a seat at the kitchen table. Michael took a seat at the far end. Any further apart, and we would've needed a telephone to conduct the meeting.

"Is your mom home?" I said.

"No."

I heard the words come pouring out from my mouth. "Great—no parents home. You have even better opportunity to frame me."

"Look—"

I kept going. "What will it be this time? Let's brainstorm together. Oh, I know—ritual sacrifice. That's it. I'm a homosexual pedophile Satanist with a taste for blood, but only during the full moon. We have to make it believable, after all."

My sarcasm was powered by real anger. Every word was edged in fury.

Michael couldn't look at me. "He made me do it," he said.

I kept my arms crossed. My face was a piece of stonework. "Nobody *made* you do anything, Michael."

"I'm sorry," he suddenly said. "Seriously. I didn't know McCauley would tell us to pretend to get sexually assaulted by you."

"Why not? He's a human-shaped sack of treachery."

"No, he's not, come on—"

I cut him off. "McCauley aims it towards a good purpose, but he's still a slimeball. I find it hard to believe that he's still a priest. You entrust your future to this guy?"

Michael was starting to cry a little. "McCauley told us to find a new sweeper. You seemed like a good fit. Plus you said you were an actor and I thought you probably needed the money."

That was a compliment. He was trying to build a bridge. I decided to set down my sledgehammer. "Thank you, but I don't appreciate being volunteered for a job without my consent."

"We can't exactly buy advertising," he replied.

That was true. I felt my defenses melting a little. The deck of cards between us began calling my name. I rapped on the table. "Okay," I said, "we'd better do this before something else happens to change my mind."

Michael eagerly shuffled the cards. I could tell he felt better to have his feet pulled out of the fire. It was starting to feel like we were on the same team.

"So you studied basic strategy," he said.

"Yeah."

"You think you're ready?"

I was getting annoyed. "Yeah. This isn't chemical engineering."

"Then show me." Michael laid out one card for himself and two for me.

Mine were a pair of sevens. His, the dealer card, was a ten.

"What do you want to do?" he said.

I thought back to the table that I had memorized. "Stand," I said proudly.

"Wrong. You hit." He swept the cards off the table. "Single deck, yes. But we're going to play multiple decks, and there are fourteen changes to basic strategy when you switch from single deck to multiple decks. McCauley's going to shred you if you don't know them."

I sighed and rubbed my eyes. "I need to study more, don't I?"

"Yeah," he said.

He went over to the modest bookshelf and pulled out a laminated document. I recognized it from watching him the other night. "Here's a better chart," he said. "On the back are all the variations for doubling and late surrender. You have to learn all of it. Don't go to McCauley until you've got this shit down. Seriously. I've seen him shoot down three other sweepers already this month."

"Fascinating," I said, stuffing it into my pocket.

He smiled. "Call me if you have questions."

Michael stood up and offered a professional handshake. This kid was reveling in his new role of authority. I would let him. After all, he would need that confidence to evade pit bosses once the gambling season began.

Leaving his apartment, I rang the wildebeest's doorbell and kept walking.

TWENTY-THREE

I lost the next two days to a haze of memorization. I photocopied the charts and pinned up the copies all over my apartment. I made up probability songs and sang them while pacing deep channels into the floor of my living room. Part of me knew that I was approaching straitjacket territory. It was easy to understand how mathematicians lost their minds.

Then I decided to practice for real. Cracking my knuckles, I opened my laptop and found a game of online blackjack and typed in my credit card number. In two hours, I lost three hundred dollars. In the next two hours, I won half of it back.

That's when I figured I was ready.

I called McCauley. He told me to meet him at a coffee shop in West Hollywood at four o'clock pm, after his high school classes let out.

I arrived twenty minutes early, and the priest was already there, waiting at a table with his hands folded, looking every centimeter the alpha male. Enhancing the effect was the woman sitting at his elbow, a sharp middle-aged blonde in a black-and-white houndstooth pantsuit. She had a black leather attaché case on her lap. Her fingers were furiously pecking at her phone.

"Jake," he said, "this is Helen. She's our chief financial officer."

That was quite a title. "It's a pleasure," I said. Helen vigorously pumped my hand twice and went back to her device.

I sat down opposite McCauley. "You've been studying?" he said.

"Harder than a third-year medical student."

He produced a deck of cards and began to shuffle them. He didn't have elderly hands. They moved deftly, nimbly. He seemed like a man in his element.

Suddenly he flicked out two cards at me. I flipped them over. A pair of eights.

"Split," I said. "Come on. A toddler could've known to do that."

"I don't know your math skills," said McCauley. He swept up the cards and reshuffled. "Try this on for size, smart guy."

He flicked two more cards at me. It was a pair of fives.

"Hit," I said.

"You don't want to split?"

I shook my head no. He grinned and swept up the cards. "Nicely done. Here's another."

The cards came skittering across the table. They were an ace and a three. But McCauley didn't turn over the hole card. "Sir," he said, imitating a dealer, "before we continue, would you like to take advantage of insurance today?"

I'd read about that. "What's the running count?"

"Plus six."

"Is the number of tens remaining greater than half the number of non-tens?"

"Excellent question," said the priest. "No, it's not."

"Then I will politely decline."

The priest nodded. "Insurance is basically giving four percent of your earnings back to the house."

As he reshuffled, Helen suddenly broke in. "I like his manners, Pat. It's important to be nice to the other players."

This surprised me. I hadn't even realized that she'd been listening.

"Why?" I asked.

"Because," the priest replied, smiling, "they're the *real* bank. It's their idiotic sacrifices that subsidize the casinos—and which we ultimately steal."

He stuffed the deck of cards into his shirt pocket. The one-on-one play was apparently over.

I felt myself growing more excited. "So I've passed?"

"Almost," he said. He pulled out several pieces of paper from his folder. "You just need to do one more thing."

Helen saw the paper and groaned. "I need to get another coffee if he's going to do *that*."

I grew alarmed. "What do I need to do?"

The old priest leaned forward. "You need to write out the entire basic strategy chart for single-deck games. Then you need to write out the entire chart for multiple-deck games. I want all variations based on doubling and early surrender."

I lowered my head. That was a large chart and would take at least twenty minutes. Michael had been right. This man was merciless.

"Okay," I said.

"You said that you'd studied."

"I have the receipt for ibuprofen to prove it."

Then his mood suddenly darkened. The priest's finger stabbed towards me, and his voice dropped to a baritone growl. "One mistake on these charts and you're gone. We never met. Is that clear, Mister Logan?"

I nodded.

"Then begin," he said.

I took a pen from my pocket. If there was any time to bail on this project, it was now. I knew the charts, but I could purposefully screw them up. Then I would be rid of McCauley's blackmail, and I could continue my life uninterrupted.

The old priest stood up from the table and picked up his attaché case.

"Aren't you going to wait?" I said.

"Hell no," McCauley said, "I've got other things to do. Helen will supervise. Hope to see you again." The old man moved behind me. I felt his hand clap me on the shoulder, then his face lower down to the side of my head. He was so close I could feel his whiskers tickling my ear. He smelled like something ancient.

"This team will save you," he whispered. "Just like it did for me."

Then the voice disappeared, the hand lifted. I whirled around. The coffee shop was full of buzzing people, but McCauley was nowhere to be seen. It was as though he'd never been there.

I sat back in my chair. It was eerie the way the old man had read my mind, the way that he'd nailed my innermost conflict. He was right: It was time to be honest with myself. Blackmail couldn't be the only glue keeping me on this team. I had to want to participate. The question was: Did I want to participate?

Yes.

The answer was unequivocal. It came from my soul.

I released my breath, picked up my pen, and began to write the charts.

TWENTY-FOUR

Forty-five minutes later, I dropped the pen and slapped the test onto Helen's table.

She had brought me a coffee and stayed nearby, conducting business on her phone. I could hear her using words that I didn't understand. Words like *savings* and *investment* and *future.*

She put on her reading glasses. "It's about time, Jake. The other candidates only took twenty minutes."

I frowned. "Maybe you should've hired them."

"McCauley didn't like them. He likes you, though. He said you don't take any shit. Is that true?"

"It depends on who's holding the shovel."

She smirked. "Give me five minutes to check your work."

I watched her begin compare my handwritten strategy chart against her own. It was going to be a meticulous job.

I stood up and crossed the coffee shop and walked into the bathroom and locked the door behind me. I turned on the water and stared at myself in the mirror.

It was time to be honest. My face was starting to show

signs of age. There were creases across my forehead, sagging of the delicate skin below the eyes. This was depressing enough for ordinary people but disastrous for actors. The likelihood of landing parts grew slimmer with every new hairline crack. I didn't look goofy enough to be a character actor either. I was powerless to stop the slide.

But Father McCauley had the power to save me.

I washed and dried my face. Then I unlocked the door with a paper towel and returned to the table.

Helen was sitting there with all the warmth of a chainsaw. I prepared for the worst.

"So what else are you doing for a living right now, Jake?" she said.

That sounded ominous. "Nothing, really."

"Good. Because you passed."

I felt a smile spread across my face like melted butter across toast. "Here," she said.

Her hand slid a small envelope across the table. I looked inside. It contained five hundred dollars.

"This is just an appetizer," she said. "We're going to give you a percentage of the winnings."

"How much?"

"To start, half a percent. When the team reaches fifty grand, we'll raise that to one percent. When the team reaches one hundred grand, it'll go to two percent. At two hundred grand, you'll get four percent. That's the ceiling."

I felt my stomach do a couple of flips. That was a nice commission structure. Four percent of two hundred grand was eight thousand dollars. And there was possibly more beyond that.

"How much did the team earn last year?" I asked.

"About six hundred, but it was a bad year. Our goal is seven hundred thousand per year."

I couldn't speak. My tongue had turned to paste. This team cleared over half a million dollars in a *slow* year. I suddenly understood why McCauley took this pursuit so seriously.

"And now it's time for your first official assignment. We are headed to the department store at the Beverly Center."

I narrowed my eyes. "Why?"

"Because I'm in charge of wardrobe, and we have to buy outfits for the boys."

I crinkled my forehead. "You can do that yourself."

She looked frustrated. "I would *love* to do it myself, but Patrick doesn't trust my judgment."

"Why?"

"I can't answer that."

That sounded like a dodge, but I let it slide. "I'm not a personal shopper, Helen."

She shook her head. "Jake, if there's one thing you should know is that McCauley is very thorough. He *always* checks up."

Our eyes locked. The five hundred dollars weighed heavy in my pocket. I thought hard, my tongue probing the inside of my cheek. "Clothes shopping? Really?"

She shrugged. It was the most sympathy I'd seen from her all afternoon. "We all wear multiple hats on this team."

Sighing, I pushed out my chair and stood up. "Let's get this over with."

TWENTY-FIVE

An hour later, I was relaxing on a bench in the men's section of the Macy's. I knew my way around this store. I'd visited these clearance racks hundreds of times. I always saw somebody that I knew. It was the proverbial water cooler for actors.

Helen held up a pair of men's pants. "What about these?"

I squinted, then shook my head. "There's a crease. Twenty-one-year-old guys don't like creases."

"You are so picky," she said.

"No, I'm an actor. I know wardrobe."

She tossed the pants aside, rummaged through a rack, and found another pair. "These look nice."

I cocked my head. She was holding up a pair of chinos. There were three pleats on each side. I almost retched. These were about as hip as a Mormon sock hop.

"You've got to be kidding me," I said.

"What? They're nice."

I suddenly understood why McCauley wanted me to accompany her on this shopping expedition. She'd probably dressed the boys the way a financial adviser and mother typically would dress a group of schoolboys. Like little job applicants from the year nineteen eighty-four.

I stood up and cracked my knuckles. "Helen, I'm going to ask you to sit down."

"Why?"

I placed a reassuring hand on her shoulder. "Because I'm going to handle this."

Her eyes burning, she stalked over to the bench and sat down. I could feel her stewing in her pique as my hands flew across the racks of fabric. It was starting to bother me.

"Helen," I said, "why don't you go and get a glass of wine or something?"

"No," she said, "one glass puts me over the edge. I don't like feeling out of control."

I didn't respond. I could feel her eyes burning a hole in my back. "My husband never bought new clothing," she said. "I had to buy everything for him."

"Where is he now?"

"Dead."

I paused. "Sorry. I didn't mean to bring it up—"

"That's how I met Patrick," she said, ignoring me. "Ten years ago he picked my son to be on the team because we were suddenly short one income."

"And you just stuck around."

"Patrick hadn't organized the team's earnings very well. He'd exposed himself to all kinds of tax liability. So I helped him reinvest, create a trust, et cetera. Now the better growth takes some of the pressure off the kids."

"So how big *is* the pot?" I asked.

"It fluctuates throughout the year. As of last week, it's about one point three million."

Holy moly. I dropped a shirt, then bent down and

picked it up.

"So how do the kids eventually get the money?"

"They don't."

"Who writes the checks to the universities?"

"We do." She looked at me with faint condescension. "You don't think that we just give a hundred fifty thousand dollars in cash to a seventeen-year-old boy, do you?"

It did sound stupid. I hadn't really thought about it.

"It's not that much work," she said. "The problem is that McCauley hasn't figured out a way for the team to earn enough to pay full tuition for all ten kids."

"So some kids gets screwed?"

"Well, we have a two-tiered structure. The first-string kids get full tuition. The second-string kids get half tuition. They're substitutes."

I'd found some fresh shirts in brightly colored stripes. The trim was standard—off-white buttons, a stray thread here and there. They looked modern and relaxed and not too expensive. Exactly what a young guy would wear to a casino.

"Those look good," I said.

"Then buy twelve," she said. "Maybe three different patterns so it's not too much of a uniform."

It was nice to see that she trusted me. I lifted the shirts off the rack and tossed them onto the floor. "So this tuition money can be used at any college?" I said.

She shook her head. "No. They have to be Jesuit colleges. That's Patrick's decision." She shrugged in a what-can-you-do manner.

"That's understandable," I said.

"It's his team. There are twenty-seven Jesuit colleges or universities in America, so the kids still have a lot of choices. And last year Patrick started the most interesting offer."

"What's that?"

"Anyone on the team who gets admitted to George-town, we cover the full tuition. Even for second string players."

I nodded. Georgetown University was the flagship Jesuit university in America. Bill Clinton had been educated there. It made sense that Patrick would be extra proud of students who attended. It also explained why Michael had said that Georgetown was his first choice. If he didn't make the first string, and if he got into Georgetown, his full tuition would be covered anyways.

"Aren't you done yet?"

I had just stumbled upon a rack of jeans that had been fashionably distressed. The price wasn't too bad either.

"These will do," I said.

"Then buy twelve," she said, without looking.

I dumped those on top of the shirts. "What about shoes?"

She waved off the question. "The boys are on their own. But I trust you'll do an inspection." She stood up. "Now, I pay—and you go home and get ready for tonight."

"What's happening tonight?"

"The final cut. We decide on the starting five. Help me carry these to the register."

Helen crouched down and lifted half the pile of cloth-ing. I lifted the other half. "How will that be done?" I asked.

"Oh, you'll see." She looked at me askance from behind the pile of pants. "Your attendance is mandatory."

That was no surprise. As I followed her through the racks, I resigned myself to the fact that my attendance on this team had been mandatory all along, even before I had known it.

TWENTY-SIX

That night, as I punched in the gate code to the rundown office complex, I saw the green, blue, red, and orange lights spinning on the plaza.

That wasn't the usual wan fluorescent drone of rental spaces. A smile cracked my face. McCauley had arranged something special.

I crossed the plaza and stepped inside the office. The old priest was standing near the door with a pair of women, one on each arm. They were young and Latina and were dressed like bar sluts. Fishnets, stretch tube tops, garish blue eyeshadow, glitter sparkling on their breasts.

They were skanks.

"Jake, I'd like you to meet Thelma and Velma," he said. "They'll be assisting us tonight."

They smiled at me but didn't speak. I could see that they were well-versed in the tricks of professional arm candy. Still, I don't like decorative women. They're like cake frosting without the cake.

"It's a pleasure," I lied.

"I bet it is," the priest said.

"Father McCauley," I shot back, "I'd like the record to show that you look like a pimp."

The priest nodded sagely. "The Lord's work takes mysterious forms." Then he nodded towards the back room. "The boys are in the back room, if you'd like to observe."

"What are they doing?"

"Trying to keep the running count. We brought in a couple of real dealers. Go back there and see if you can spot which kid is counting."

I walked past him, the skanks smiling at me, towards the flashing blue, green, red, and orange lights in the back room I stepped inside.

The classical music was gone, replaced by pulsing dance music kept at ambient levels. The round tables on which we'd eaten dinner were gone. In their place, two green semicircular blackjack tables had been erected. Five boys were arranged around each one, while two tuxedoed dealers flipped out cards. The dealers wore impassive looks on their faces.

I leaned against the wall and watched the boys. Michael was trying his best to have a good time, joshing his buddy next to him. After all, half his college tuition depended upon his performance that evening.

Then I noticed Helen standing nearby. In her hands was a clipboard. She was watching the boys intently. Occasionally she made a note.

I slid my back alongside the wall towards her. "So I think that one is counting."

"Which one?"

I nodded towards a kid perched on a stool. He was sitting very, very still—not a twitch. His scared eyes darted to every overturned card on the table. He looked like a frightened little fish.

Helen frowned. "Duh."

"Hey, I'm new at this."

"Fair enough," she said. "At least he's not moving his lips. That's an automatic disqualification."

I looked at the pile of chips in front of each kid. "Do they all get a chance to count?"

"Yeah, we're on the last pair before Patrick brings in the girls." She paused, her ears pricked up. "Oh, here come the ladies of the evening."

The clicking and clacking sound of stiletto heels came echoing down the hard floor of the hallway. Then I felt something soft brush the back of my arm. I turned and made eye contact with Velma—or maybe it was Thelma. It didn't really matter. She was holding a server's tray.

The spandexed floozies began to cozy up to the teenage boys. They cooed, tittered, tried to ask questions. One even tried to steal some chips. They'd had a lot of practice doing this.

As the girls went from boy to boy, each reacted differently. Some exhibited better self-control and treated the women with amused mastery. Some were embarrassed and couldn't speak. Others responded with shining eyes and disbelief at their good fortune. I could almost hear the pant fabric expanding.

McCauley arrived alongside Helen and watched the scene with an impassive eye. He occasionally pointed to something on her clipboard.

I craned my head. "How do they look?"

McCauley shook his head. "Poor impulse control in seven of ten. It's going to be a bad year."

"You want them to ignore the girls, right?"

"Not entirely," said McCauley. "That would draw the attention of the pit boss. The most promising ones know how to balance their attention. Only Colman's really doing it right."

"Oh God," said Helen. A look of motherly concern passed across her face. "Look."

I followed her gaze. One boy with eyes like a pair of knife slits had slipped his hand onto Velma's buttock. She wasn't stopping him.

"That's Seth," she said. "Why did you take him, Patrick?"

McCauley stroked his chin. "His dad abandoned the family three years ago. And the science department tells me he's great at biology. This country needs more researchers."

Helen wasn't convinced. "He's going to be the biggest problem. Mark my words."

I thought back to my own teenage years and decided to play the other angle. "Well, he *is* seventeen years old."

"That's exactly the problem," she replied.

"Isn't that old enough?"

"You're not a mother."

I shrugged and looked at the other players. At the other table, Michael was ignoring the other skank's come-ons. He was paying more attention to the cards.

I nudged McCauley. "Hey, what's the verdict on Michael?"

"Second string," said the priest. "He's made too many mistakes tonight. Right now, he's got counter written all over him."

I felt bad. That meant half a college education. Tens of thousands of dollars gone—poof—down the drain. Just for ignoring a skanky girl.

Soon, I sensed that nobody really needed me here. That's when McCauley turned to me. "I'm going to ask you to conduct a workshop tomorrow night."

"For what?"

"Every year, we spend one session showing the kids how to be manly," he said.

I laughed. "Really?"

"Don't laugh. It's not as easy as it seems. We teach them how to walk, talk, carry themselves. Some kids figure it out early. Others don't figure it out at all. The point is that they need to fool the pit bosses into thinking they're of age."

"And you want me to teach them how to be men?"

"Yeah."

"Why don't you do it?"

McCauley looked sad. "I'm a seventy-seven-year-old priest. You figure it out."

Helen added, "Multiple hats, Jake—remember?"

I glanced at the boys. I'd done stupider things. This would be a good way to build their respect for me.

TWENTY-SEVEN

Twenty-four hours later.

I was in the same back room, doing my best General Patton, marching back and forth in front of a line of teenage boys. They watched me with amusement.

"Okay, ladies," I said, "let's see what you've learned in two hours of finishing school."

I'd researched and planned this little session all day. "Perry," I said, "tell me what we've learned about manliness."

Perry cleared his throat. "Um ... no sudden movements."

I nodded. "Who's a good example of this?"

"Old men," he said.

"Arthritis prohibits jerkiness," I said, "one of the ironic benefits of getting old. Samuel, how do we walk into a room?"

"Shoulders first," came the answer.

"Michael, are you ever friends with a girl whom you secretly like?"

"No, sir," came the reply.

"Why not?"

"Because the friend zone is deadly, sir."

"Samuel, on a scale of 1 to 10, with a nice guy being a 1 and an asshole being a 10, what number do we aim for?"

"Six," he replied.

"Seven if you're in a bad mood," I added. "What drink do you order from the cocktail waitress at the casinos?"

"Mineral water with lime," he said.

"Why?"

"Because you can tell people it's a screwdriver."

"No, a gin and tonic. Study harder."

I smacked him on the knee. He buried his head in his hands.

"Gentlemen," I said, "you may be good at math, but you've got to change your demeanors in a hurry to pull this off. All right, we're done. Don't forget to text me the pictures of the shoes you're planning to buy before you purchase them. Seth, what's the description?"

"No sneakers."

"And thin soles. Dismissed."

The boys wearily shuffled out of the room. Michael smiled at me on his way out. "Nice work, man."

"Thank you."

"I didn't realize you could be authoritative."

"I'm an actor," I said. "I can be whatever people ask me to be."

As I packed up my things, I noticed that one other person had remained behind. It was Colman, the quietest student. He had a slight build, narrow shoulders. I noticed that he always paid careful attention to my words.

"Jake," he said, "I'm having real trouble with these manliness tips."

"Just practice them until they become second nature," I said. "You'll get the hang of it."

"No, I can't," he said. Something in his voice caught my ear. I sensed that there was something else at work here. Something that preferred show tunes and pert bottoms.

"Ah," I said, "now it makes sense."

"What does?"

"The fact that you like guys."

Yep, I put it out there. His eyes grew huge. "That's not true."

"Oh, come on. You naturally walk with your tummy out. No straight guy does that." I softened. "Don't worry. I won't tell anybody."

He seemed to deflate. "You're the first person who ever guessed."

"Doubtful."

Colman loosened up. Underneath the mannerisms, I could see that he was actually tough. "Jake, half this stuff just isn't right for me."

"Like what?"

"Like owning a room. You know? What should *I* do?"

I understood his dilemma. I also understood why McCauley hadn't sent him to the gym that fateful night the previous week.

I leaned against the edge of a desk and stroked my chin. "Well," I said, "I could try to teach you how to be a sophisticated adult gay man."

"You're not gay."

"I have friends."

His eyes were suddenly shining, and I hastened to correct myself. "All I'm saying is that I can give you some tips."

The kid nodded. "That would help a lot." He started to

leave, then stopped. His eyes were full of anxiety. "Do we have to tell the team?"

"No, let's keep it our secret."

As Colman left the room, I had a strange feeling in my stomach, something that I hadn't felt in years of working on dog-eat-dog production sets.

I had started to feel like a part of a team.

TWENTY-EIGHT

McCauley announced the first-string team the next night. Then he announced that our first trip was going to occur the following Thursday. Full practice sessions were set for the next six nights.

Each night, I arrived at the office at exactly seven o'clock for a catered dinner on chinaware. Over the years, McCauley said, he'd discovered that porcelain somehow made teenage boys behave more maturely.

Then everybody cleared the dishes, washed them. Others folded the tables. Still others dragged over the green semicircular blackjack tables.

Then the group split. At one table, Helen served as dealer to the second string. The den mother flipped cards around the table like a professional. I wondered if she'd ever been a card-counter the way McCauley had.

At the other table, McCauley dealt to the first-string players. He was as strict as any drill instructor. I watched him closely. His eyes flitted around, from player, to cards, to players, back to cards. Nothing escaped his gaze.

"Seth," he said, "sit up, you're slouching too much. They'll think you're drunk."

Then McCauley's eyes went to the next boy. "You, Samuel, pull the umbrella out of your ass and relax. They'll think you're cheating."

The boy tried to smile. Then the priest abruptly stopped dealing and pointed to Perry.

"What's the count?"

Perry stammered. "P ... p... plus ... four."

The old priest shook his head. "No, it's plus three. That's strike one."

I learned that McCauley kept a three-strikes-and-you're-out rule. For players on the first string, three mistakes in practice meant you lost your place. Sometimes the priest demoted after only two strikes. Nobody complained.

I started to understand the method behind the madness. It was the same tactics used by great coaches and teachers. Keep shifting, stay three steps ahead of your players, hand out demotions and promotions with the same wolf-like, inscrutable arbitrariness—and your players and students will both fear and respect you.

Most importantly, they would perform better.

Occasionally McCauley would point at me and say, "Disruption, please." I'd stagger over, pretending to be drunk, lean over the boys, and jabber about nothing at all. It was fun pretending to be loud and ignorant. My goal was to make the boys screw up the running count.

They deserved a good laugh. After all, they worked hard. I was in awe of the speed of their mental processing. I sometimes stood behind them and tried to follow along with their card counting. It made my eyeballs ache.

One night, McCauley suddenly put down the cards and motioned to Helen to stop dealing. "Gentlemen, we have one thing left to do," he announced. "It involves our sweeper."

My heart leapt in my chest. I'd been waiting for this.

"Can you guess what it might be?" he said.

Chris raised his hand. "We need to alert him somehow that the count is high or low."

"Exactly," said the priest. "How we do that is up to you. Take five minutes and decide."

He stepped away from the table, hands up in penitence. This was his way of allowing the boys to cement their bond.

The teenagers were happy for the break. They filed out of the office and into the plaza. I followed, listening to the discussion about the best way to signal me. Someone suggested throwing a napkin into the air. Someone else suggested saying the word "and" for a plus count, "but" for a minus count, and the number. Others involved thumps and slaps in certain order.

I stepped forward and raised my voice. "There's too much that can go wrong. We should just use simple body language."

"Like what?" said Michael.

"I don't know. Maybe stretching?"

That started a discussion. The boys agreed that they would need to stretch after an hour of sitting at a blackjack table.

"The word *left* comes from the Latin word for *sinister*," said Samuel. "Maybe twisting to the left could mean a minus count. You know, like—stay away."

"And twisting right could mean a plus count," added Perry. "Each bounce indicates how high the plus count is. Like this." He placed his hands on his hips and twisted to the right, bouncing five times. "Plus five. It's easy."

"But we need a way to get Jake over to the table," said Michael.

"Just lean back and stretch with your arms up in the air," I answered. "Lace your fingers together. It'll get my attention because it's a big, tall movement."

I demonstrated. Michael clapped. "That's good. It works. Everybody agree?"

There were murmurs of approval. "McCauley's going to love it," said Samuel.

"I already do," said the priest. We all spun around. The old Jesuit had been standing inside the office door, watching and listening.

"Father McCauley," I said, "this team is ready. You've prepped them and drilled them."

"Maybe," he said. "Everybody take tomorrow off. On Friday, be here immediately after school. The van leaves at three-thirty pm."

"Where are we going?" he said.

The priest smiled, but his eyes were dark pools of mystery. "To our first casino."

TWENTY-NINE

That Friday, when I pulled up to the office, a fourteen-passenger van was idling on the street outside the office. Helen sat behind the wheel.

"I didn't bring an overnight bag," I said.

"You won't need it," she replied. "The first one is always a quick dine-n-dash. We'll be home by midnight."

"Where are we going?"

"A little crappy casino out near San Bernardino. They have a five-dollar minimum."

"Is it a good place?"

She hemmed and hawed. "It's a good place to start. Most places have a ten-dollar minimum."

The boys had started to arrive and were climbing into the van. "Where's McCauley?" I said.

"Inside."

"I can drive, if you need me to."

"Not unless you have a Class B driver's license," she replied. "Otherwise the state won't let you operate one of these things." She jerked a thumb backwards. "Get in with the boys."

As I climbed inside, Michael was already waiting on one of the bench seats. I slid in next to him. "Nervous?" I said.

"Nah," he replied. "I'm second string. All I do is make conversation and play basic strategy on small bets."

Soon McCauley came out of the office. He stumbled on the edge of lawn and leaned against an oak tree. He seemed suddenly older. I guessed that, at age seventy-seven, good health was a day-to-day affair. The old priest yanked open the door and fell awkwardly into the passenger seat.

When his breathing had calmed down, he looked at Helen. "Everybody accounted for?"

"Yes," said Helen.

"Who was the last to arrive?"

"You were," I said.

The old priest twisted around and pointed at me. "Strike one," he said. I couldn't tell if it was a joke.

Helen started the engine, put the van into drive, and pulled out into traffic. A few minutes later, we were on the freeway. McCauley reached into the bag on the floor near his feet. "Gentlemen," he said, "courtesy of Helen, it is now Christmas morning. Pass these around, one a piece."

He passed ten envelopes to the back of the van. The teenagers excitedly ripped them open. Each one contained cash.

"Only two hundred dollars?" said Michael.

"At five dollars per minimum bet," said the McCauley, "that's forty hands, even if you don't win a single one. Most of you should go sixty to eighty hands. That's enough to get a count going."

Nobody responded. The visceral excitement of being given two hundred dollars of someone else's money was being replaced by the sinking feeling that it was someone else's money.

"Now put the cash in your wallets," he said. "We don't want ten kids in a row at the cashier pulling money out of identical envelopes."

The kids folded the money into their pockets, then lapsed into silence. We listened to the shush of the rubber tires on the road. I stared out the window and thought about my marginal life. Most people got a job in an organization and progressed upwards as the years passed. My life, however, had been a series of random events. I'd been an actor, a tutor, and now a professional card counter.

The shape of my life wasn't an incline slope. It was a scatterplot.

Two hours later, we pulled off the freeway and wound through the streets of San Bernardino. McCauley was consulting his map. "Pull over here," he suddenly said.

We were on an ordinary four-lane street. Helen pulled the van over into a metered parking spot and shut off the engine.

"Is this it?" said Samuel.

"Yes," said McCauley. "The casino should be about four blocks down."

"Why can't we park at the casino?"

"They have security cameras in the garage. We don't want them getting the license plate of this van."

That made sense. I realized that we were operating on the shady side of the law. The sunset through the tree limbs sent an orange shaft of light into my eyes. It felt like the judgment of God. I used a hand to shield my face.

The boys had begun grumbling.

"You're young, you can walk four blocks," said the priest. "So here's how we work it. Each member of the first string partners with a member of the second string." He read the names of the pairs off his clipboard. He'd worked this out ahead of time.

"You guys are buddies tonight. You sit at the same table, next to one another. First string guy does the counting, second string watches the staff, makes conversation. Nobody bets more than the minimum."

"Seriously?" said Seth.

"Yes," said McCauley. "Have you been listening at all for the last two months? We are *steaming*. That means, camouflage your counting with consistently small wagers. What that means is simple. I don't care if the count goes to plus nine, *you place the five-dollar minimum*. No exceptions. The only person who's going big here is Jake."

Helen interrupted. "And choose tables far from one another. You don't want to appear to be in any way related."

McCauley lifted a warning finger. "Lastly, I need to remind you that there are three easy ways for any of you to get kicked off the team. First, drink alcohol. Second, speak to Jake at the table. Third, bet more than the minimum. If any of these things occur, you will not receive any funds for college. Am I being clear?"

The boys murmured in response. I could sense their fear. Then Michael raised his hand timidly.

"Yes, Michael."

"Are you gambling tonight, Father McCauley?"

"Hell no," he answered. "The great and powerful Oz stays behind his curtain. You boys are on your own."

"Is Helen coming?" said Perry.

She looked up. "No, I always stay here and listen to Patrick snore. Good luck, everybody."

"We don't need luck," said McCauley. "That's why we *count*. Now, gentlemen, go and make some money."

The boys didn't move. The atmosphere was tense. This felt like the kickoff before the first game of the season.

I reached over and popped open the door. "I'll see you soon, guys."

Finally, the teenagers began to squeeze out of the van. When the last one had left, I slammed the door shut. Now there was only McCauley, Helen, and myself remaining.

We watched the ten boys shuffle down the sidewalk and disappear. "What do you think?" I asked. "Are they ready?"

The old priest shrugged. "It depends upon the personalities. There's always one who surprises me." He looked at me in the rearview mirror. "What about you? Do you feel ready?"

"Sure," I said.

"No mistakes tonight?"

"None."

"Good. Here." He handed me another envelope. I looked inside. It contained a thousand dollars. "Just play the charts. Be sure to hit all five tables. Lay down a hundred dollars on a plus count and ride that bitch until the dealer reshuffles. Lay down seventy on the minus count and quit the table after three hands."

I was confused. "Shouldn't I just skip the cold tables?"

His reddened eyes gazed sadly at me in the mirror. "Jake, casino databases are stuffed with the pictures of counters who got too greedy. If you want any longevity, you have to lose too."

"Oh," I said.

"It's very Biblical," he continued. "You know—the meek shall inherit the earth." The priest waved his hand dismissively.

I checked my watch. "So how long do I wait?"

"Give them a good thirty minutes. A couple will prob-ably poop their little pants anyways."

I leaned back in his seat. Soon McCauley was snoring. Helen had donned her glasses and was reading an economics magazine.

Sitting alone on the back bench, I felt about as useful as a paper wrench. I opened the door, stepped outside, and headed towards the casino.

THIRTY

I sauntered down the sidewalk, hands in my pockets, mentally preparing for the character. The process felt identical to what I'd done preparing for roles in television productions.

After all, I'd learned the story (blackjack). I'd understood my place inside of the script (the team). I'd memorized my lines (basic strategy).

Now I was imagining a backstory for myself. I was supposed to be a bit of a high roller, an image that was challenging to project without money, clothing, women, or friends. So instead I'd be a lone wolf, one with lots of practice playing online, who'd mastered basic strategy, and who was having an exceptionally good night. I'd accept the free drinks and get happier as the chips piled up. That wouldn't be hard. I'd honestly be feeling great.

The casino came into view. It was midcentury construction with a swooping roof and brick lattice wall painted white. A pair of tiny pink spotlights shone onto the sign: *The San Bernardino Casino*. It was about as glamorous as a ninety-year-old movie star.

I aimed my shoes towards the main portico and sauntered inside. The stale smell of old cigarettes assaulted my
nose. A cracked staircase led up to the gaming floor. And to
the wall on my right, beneath a line of yellowish water
damage, was the row of cashier's windows.

I approached one of the tellers. He seemed to be
approaching the century mark. The elderly man was
leaning forward with his chin propped up on one hand. His
eyes were shut and his lower jaw was slightly to the left of
his mouth. It would shift whichever way gravity was
headed.

"Good morning, sunshine," I said.

His eyes creaked open. They were blue and rheumy.
"There ain't nobody good here," he said.

"You guys have got some money that needs loosening," I
said.

"Like my stools," he said.

This man was going to bring down my spirits. I slid my
money across the table to him. "It's a thousand dollars," I
said.

He rang up the exchange, then pushed the chips
towards me wordlessly. He'd probably done a lot bigger
exchanges. I suddenly felt irrelevant.

"Thank you," I said.

He didn't reply. The chin had landed on the palm
again, and the eyes had squinched shut.

I stuffed the chips into my pockets and headed up the
stairs. My shoes felt like they weighed twenty pounds each.
I'd told myself not to feel nervous. My body wasn't
listening.

One thing I hadn't told McCauley was that this was my
first time in a casino. At the top of the stairs, I paused and

looked around. Before me was a wide expanse of slot machines.

I wandered through the field of endless sounds and colors and felt sick to my stomach. The players themselves looked like husks of humans for whom life had ended long ago. Many in fact looked sick, oxygen tanks nearby, credit cards on lanyards around their necks. Their financial bankruptcy matched their spiritual bankruptcy.

I glimpsed the blackjack tables and dashed over, thankful to escape the slot zombies. I checked my watch. It'd been thirty minutes since the boys had left the van. I would make a pass through the areas, scope out the tables, silently announce my presence to the boys, and wait for that first stretch.

I entered the blackjack area. There were about fifteen different tables in play. I quickly spotted the boys.

It didn't take long to get the first signal. A pair of long arms stretched up towards the ceiling. They belonged to Perry. Then I saw him twist to the right, and bounce—once, twice, three times.

That meant the count was plus three. It was show time.

THIRTY-ONE

I pulled a cigarette from my pocket and lit it and took a drag. I'm not a smoker, but back in the day, actors had to know how to smoke well. Fondling a cigarette gave us something to do with our hands during scenes.

I swaggered across the room, nodding at people, making eye contact, pausing at a table, then deciding against it, teasing other players—and finally flitting over, almost randomly, to a seat at Perry and Samuel's table.

The two teenagers glanced at me nervously. Of course they would be nervous. They were underage, were in possession of fake IDs, and were counting cards at blackjack.

"I like the feeling of this table," I said. "This feels good to me. Yessir. Let's do a hundred."

I placed four green chips on the table in front of me. The dealer flipped out the cards. Mine were a jack and a queen.

I had twenty. Almost the best hand you can get. The dealer was showing a six.

"I will stand, my friend," I ordered the dealer. "Now,

stand and deliver."

"Ho boy," said the woman next to me. She had envy slathered like suntan lotion across her reddened face. "You must be a psychic to sit down here and get a twenty right off the bat."

I shrugged. "It's just my night, ma'am. I can feel it." The words sounded ridiculous, worse than most of the dialogue I'd been hired to read on camera, but people really believed this stuff. I could feel myself falling into the clichés.

The hole card was a seven. The dealer made it to fifteen —and then busted. I expelled a breath. I'd just won a hundred dollars. The dealer pushed four more green chips across the felt. A bolt of excitement coursed through my body. This was the adrenalin rush that kept so many millions of people coming back to the casinos. The entire gaming industry was built upon the squirts of this chemical.

"Let's do it again," I said. "I like this table."

I shoveled over four more green chips. This time I had a two and a king. This was a twelve. There was about an even chance of getting a face card now, since the count was high. "Hit," I said.

He sent me another card. It was another king. Twenty-two. I busted.

Instantly I felt a flood of panic. I'd just lost a hundred dollars. Granted, I'd only had that money for a minute, but I felt the pain anyways. I reminded myself of the study that McCauley had showed me. It revealed that humans feel losses three times more acutely, in a physiological sense, than they feel wins.

I ignored my feelings and went back to the game.

The dealer took the four chips back. I placed my original four chips back on the square. This time, he dealt me a pair of nines. He was showing a face card.

"Let's split," I said.

I separated my one hand into two hands. The dealer handed me two more cards, one for each. I turned them over. They were both face cards. Now I had two hands worth nineteen each.

"You son of a bitch," said the woman next to me. She had busted.

"Life can be good," I said. "It's rainbows and butterflies and lollipops, if you want it to be."

"Not mine," she said.

I held my breath as the dealer flipped over his hole card. If it was a nine, I would get a push, which meant a draw—the bet would be returned to me. If it were an eight or less, I would get the full amount of winning.

It was an eight.

I beat my hands in the air, a joyous expression of sheer exuberance. I wasn't acting either. The dealer's mouth curled into a small expression of something like admiration. "Congratulations."

He pushed eight more green chips across the felt. I had just won two hundred dollars. I looked at Perry and Samuel. They were looking at me with a mixture of admiration, awe, and relief. Their stacks of chips was running dangerously low. Keeping the running count carried a price.

I calmed myself down. This was their money, earned through months of sweat, toil, and mathematical discipline. I hadn't done anything except play the cards straight for a couple minutes.

I took out a stack of five-dollar red chips. I handed the dealer a couple, then I tossed one to each of the other players at the table. Perry and Samuel caught theirs in midair. "Better luck next time."

THIRTY-TWO

Ninety minutes later, I slid open the back door of the van and hopped inside. All the boys were assembled inside. The sour smell of adolescent underarm stink was mixed with the smell of spilled liquor.

"It's been a good night, fellas," I said.

"So how much did we make?" said Michael.

"Guess," I said.

I settled back and listened to the estimates. *Six hundred. Thirteen hundred. Two thousand seventy-four.*

As directed, I'd visited all their tables that night. The counts had ranged from plus five to minus four, and I'd played the cards exactly as told, using basic strategy.

"The total is three thousand one hundred forty dollars," I said. "Congratulations, you guys."

The boys burst out into spontaneous applause. McCauley even turned around. "You broke three thousand?"

"Yep," I said proudly.

"On those tables? In ninety minutes?"

I nodded smugly.

McCauley seemed a little surprised. "That's better than I'd expected."

"You stayed at my table for a really long time," said Colman. "You knew it was minus four, right?"

I'd lost nearly five hundred dollars at his table. "Of course," I replied. "Didn't I look sad enough?"

"Dude, I thought you were really going to cry," came the reply. "Seriously, you looked so depressed."

"Thank you," I said proudly.

"I was watching the pit boss too," said Samuel. "As soon as you lost that first hand, he turned away."

"Really?" I said.

We all looked at McCauley with newfound respect. Everything he'd been telling us about the process had been turning out to be dead on. He knew exactly how to earn a fortune at gambling. You just had to be sneaky enough, disciplined enough, and humble enough.

I handed McCauley the envelope with the winnings. Helen gunned the motor, and the van roared to life. "Anybody hungry?" said Helen.

The teenagers roared yes. I smiled. I was getting hungry too as the adrenaline began to subside.

"You have to wait twenty minutes," she said. "We need to get out of San Bernardino first."

She put us back on the freeway, drove about twenty miles, then exited to an In-N-Out Burger. That was safe. I've never met anybody in Los Angeles who disliked that chain.

We piled out of the van and ran inside. We let the boys order first. McCauley picked up the tab for the whole group at the cash register.

I was just about to sit down, alone in a red plastic booth, when the priest beckoned at me. "Over here, Jake," he said.

I joined him and Helen at their booth. They each had a cup of coffee before them, looking like bored chaperones, which they were.

I dropped my tray on the table and slid into the seat. "What's up?"

McCauley had placed his special reading glasses on his nose. "As you know, we were talking to the boys before you got back to the van."

I had picked up my hamburger but set it down again. I'd lost my appetite. Beginning a conversation with the words *As you know* didn't bode well.

"And?" I said.

"And I want to review some of your decisions." The old man's eyes roved across his clipboard. "Samuel says that you doubled down on an eighteen to the dealer's ten and lost."

I remembered that. It'd been my biggest loss of the night. "So?"

"The count was plus four."

"You told me to just play basic strategy," I said.

He grew impatient. "Yes, but you need to think strategically too, since you have knowledge that other players don't."

"Explain it to me."

I could tell that he was getting frustrated. "Look, basic strategy says that four-thirteenths of the cards are face cards. But you know that if the count is plus four, there's more than that remaining, proportionally—in fact at plus four there's probably a shitload of face cards coming up. So you'd better think long and hard about doubling down on an eighteen when the dealer is showing a ten. You understand that?"

He was right. I nodded.

He sighed loudly. "Jake, I told you to just play basic

strategy because it's your first time out. I thought you would be smart enough to calibrate. But according to what the boys told me, you cost us five hundred dollars."

I blanched. The way he'd phrased that, McCauley made me sound unbelievably irresponsible.

"I did?" It came out like a croak.

Helen added: "That's worth, after ten years' compound interest, about a thousand dollars."

McCauley nodded. "That's half the cost of a college course."

I looked down at my hands. This was a big piece of humble pie.

He softened. "Hand to hand, the boys can win or lose, and it doesn't affect the team much. Tonight, they happened to do well—they won about seven hundred dollars overall."

"That's great," I said.

He leaned forward. "But their bets don't matter, Jake. Only *yours* do. You have to play *perfect* cards. There's no room for error. These boys and their families are depending upon you."

"Okay," I said.

He jabbed a finger at me. "That's strike two, Jake. Next time, you're out. Hear me?"

His eyes held mine to let me know that he was serious. The gauntlet had been thrown. The thought of being tossed off the team sent a stabbing pain through my chest. I'd become hooked, and McCauley knew it.

"I'll make up for it next time," I promised.

"You'd better," he said. "Now, here's your portion of the night's proceedings."

He peeled off several bills and slid them across the table at me. It was a hundred dollars.

"Not bad for two hours' work," said Helen. She was trying to put a bright face on the conversation. "There should be even more next time."

I smiled wanly, then put the cash in my pocket. I lifted my tray and moved to another nearby table to lick my wounds.

I could feel the strange gravity of this priest, this sorcerer of probability, dragging me further down the rabbit hole.

THIRTY-THREE

Four days later, the card-counting team took its next trip—
this time to a casino up in Ventura.

It was the same scenario. Meet at the office, pile into the
van, drive for two hours.

Sandwiched between Michael and Samuel, I watched
McCauley's graying hair sway above the seat ahead of me.
This time, I vowed to play the cards perfectly.

I leaned forward and tugged on his sleeve. "Father
McCauley?" I said.

"What?" He turned his head.

I peered over his shoulder. He was holding a small silver
flask discreetly between his legs. I decided to pretend that I
hadn't seen it. "Tell me about the strategy," I said.

"Tell you what?"

"Are there any changes?"

"Well, the minimum bet here is ten dollars, instead of
five."

"What does that mean for me?"

He twisted around slightly. "The maximum bet is
usually twenty times greater than the minimum. That's why

I instructed you to bet a hundred on a five-dollar table. But tonight we go bigger. I want you to bet one fifty up to plus three, and the full two hundred if the count goes any higher."

That got me feeling a bit nervous. Betting two hundred dollars per hand made me question my own skills.

He seemed to read my mind. "I have confidence in you," he said. "And there's a lot of money in this one for you —if you don't mess up."

I thought of the past due slip that had been taped to my door the previous week. My landlord had reached his breaking point. "I'll play perfect cards this time."

"Let's hope so."

"Promise."

We pulled off the freeway slipped through the beach-side town of Ventura. I'd heard a lot about this town, how people who couldn't stand the density and congestion of Los Angeles moved here. It did seem relaxed. Quiet blue bungalows, modest condos, streetlights that seemed to linger on red forever. I'd thought about moving here, once. But I know myself. I'd get bored in a small town.

Helen stopped the van a few blocks away. "Two hours, boys," said McCauley, "and that's it. Now let's say a quick Our Father."

The boys dropped their heads and followed him in reciting the Lord's Prayer. I followed along, not wanting to feel out of place. When they had finished, Father McCauley made the sign of the cross.

"Now get your asses into that casino and start counting."

The boys left the van in five waves. I followed behind, the sixth wave.

The Ventura Star Casino looked better than the one in

San Bernardino. It was a stucco box, true, but there was no visible water damage on this one. A double row of king palms lined the front walkway, each lit by a red, white, or blue floodlight.

My fingers dragged along the scratchy trunks as I passed down the walk. At the entrance of the casino, a doorman opened the door for me. I thought about tipping him ten dollars but decided against it. My acting should only go so far.

I found the cashiers. The windows were framed in freshly polished brass. And the cashiers weren't falling asleep on their hands. This was a step up.

I looked inside the envelope that McCauley had given me. There was three thousand dollars. My sphincter clenched. The old priest was expecting me to swing for the fences. I couldn't disappoint him.

I stepped up to the window and quickly traded the money for a pile of forty chips. Twenty hundreds and twenty fifties. It was a surprisingly small cache for such a large amount of money.

I dumped the chips into the pockets of my coat and headed through a low-ceilinged hallway and emerged onto the casino floor. The usual expanse of dead-eyed slot monsters beckoned to my right. I'd had enough of them at the last casino. They made my soul cry.

The blackjack tables were to the left—at least fifty of them. This was a bigger place. I decided to make an early pass, to see if anybody was ready to signal me yet.

I saw the boys at various tables, chatting, laughing, sipping mineral waters. All was orderly. Nobody signaled me yet.

With nothing better to do, I headed over to the bar and

ordered a Scotch. It's my favorite old man drink. I don't care who knows it.

A mane of blonde hair flashed in my peripheral vision. I glanced over. She was a cougar. I'd figured that they would hang out here. This one was trying to nonchalantly signal to me. The problem was that her skin told me that she catnapped in a tanning bed.

She twinkled her fingers at me, then pawed her platinum blonde hair. This wasn't fair. I was too young for her. I didn't have time tonight to toy with her either.

About five tables down, a pair of outstretched arms caught my other eye. It was Colman. He twisted right and bounced six times. Plus six. My stomach plunged into my shoes.

I swallowed my drink, ambled across the carpet, and chose a seat at his table. Colman was dressed fabulously in a low-cut purple t-shirt and skinny jeans and an expensive-looking bracelet. He tried to acknowledge me with a nod. I ignored him. My character would feel uncomfortable around underage twinks.

I reached into my pocket and placed two black chips on the baize felt. "This shit better work," I said. "My ex tells me that my kids need some new school clothes this weekend."

The female dealer didn't respond. I was getting the sense that dealers had their personalities surgically removed prior to hiring. "Would you like to buy insurance?" she said.

"Hell no," I spat.

She passed out the cards. Mine were an ace and a jack—a natural, twenty-one, the best possible hand. I whooped out loud. "That's the shit," I said, "right there. Hoo-boy."

The dealer, however, was showing a jack. While the others hit, I licked my chops. This would be good.

She flipped her hole card. It was an ace. The dealer had blackjack too. I groaned theatrically. "Why, darling, why oh why … do you have to steal my thunder?"

"It's just my job," she said.

"Wait 'til I get a few more cocktails in me, you won't know what hit you." I drummed my thumbs on the table. "What's taking so long?"

The next cards hurtled across the felt. They were a queen and a three. The dealer was showing a two. This was a terrible hand when the count was a plus six. I glanced at the shoe of cards. It was almost bursting with face cards. The dealer would most likely bust. I would too.

"Stand," I said.

"On a thirteen?" said the dealer.

I shrugged. "I just feel weird about this one. Kinda like how I felt when I saw my ex-wife for the first time."

She shrugged and flipped her hole card. It was a ten. Now she had twelve. She took another card. It was another ten.

Busted.

"Bet you had a funny feeling it would be a bust," said the dealer, pushing two more black chips across the table towards me.

"God, I wish I'd had that feeling when I first saw my ex-wife," I cracked.

She didn't respond. I played five more hands and won four. Other players had started to gather behind me. When a table gets hot, other players figure it out.

Then I felt a hand on my shoulder. I started to panic. I wasn't ready to talk to a pit boss. I hadn't done anything wrong.

It wasn't a pit boss. It was the blonde cougar from the bar. "Hey Jack," she said, "you're doing *fantastic*." Her eyes were fixed upon my pile of black chips. I'd won a thousand dollars' worth in less than fifteen minutes.

"Well thank you," I said.

"If it's all right with you, I'm just going to stand here and see how you do what you do," she said. Her hand stayed on my shoulder. Her fingertips started to caress my neck.

I felt my concentration begin to waver. I couldn't focus with this woman hovering over me like a money-slurping vacuum.

Then I saw Colman twist to the right. He made eight tiny bounces to the right.

Holy shit. This deck was beyond hot.

Behind the dealer, a heavy man in a suit was watching the table closely. He was wearing an earpiece.

The platinum blonde had squeezed between me and the next player and thrown her arm around my shoulders. Her fake breasts were jammed in my face. She was trying to point to something on the table. "Show me how you do this? How many of those do you get?"

I looked at the dealer, who glanced at the aging vixen but said nothing.

Suddenly I couldn't take it anymore. There was too much pressure here, too many unexplained variables. "You know what," I said, disentangling myself, "I gotta hit the head."

The dealer said, "Do you want me to hold your place?"

"No," I said, "I think I've milked this table enough."

I scooped the chips into my pocket and set off across the casino floor to the men's room. I went into a toilet stall and locked it behind me and stood there.

McCauley hadn't been kidding. You really needed to keep your focus to succeed at a blackjack table.

THIRTY-FOUR

A few minutes later, I emerged from the bathroom and scanned the room. The cougar was nowhere to be found. But I did find Samuel signaling a plus two. I sidled over, took a stool, did my usual thing.

After my third winning hand, the cougar reappeared at my side. Her face looked even more glossy, her eyes even more lit up. "There you are," she said. "You can't lose me, honey. I'm just going to keep standing right here by your side and watch you work your magic."

I noticed that she had a slight Southern lilt. She'd probably been a beauty queen at her high school, moved out to California to model, gotten sidetracked, and was now a casino floozy.

"Where I come from," I said, "women make themselves useful."

She stared at me. "Oh my goodness, me just standin' here while you're winning all this *money*. I know what I'm going to do—I'm going to get you a *drink*."

The cougar left and came back in less than two minutes

with a glass of brown liquid. "I noticed you drinking this earlier," she said.

"You're friendly," I said.

"My momma always said that," came the reply.

I sniffed the glass; it was another scotch. I frowned but accepted the drink. Across the table, Samuel was trying not to laugh.

The game continued, and as I kept winning, the cougar edged in closer and closer, skin on skin. I bore down on the cards. It was a relief when the dealer announced that it was time to reshuffle. I took my winnings and stood up. Nearby, I saw Seth signaling plus three.

I shuffled over and began playing there. The cougar materialized after my very first hand. Her hand felt icy cold on my shoulder.

I removed the hand and turned to face her full-on. "Miss Sparkle, I'm gonna need you to back off for a little."

"Why?"

"You're scaring off the younger women. You know, the ones I want to sleep with."

I thought that would cut her to her soul, but her eyes stayed oddly aglow. Nothing indicated that she'd heard my dig. "Honey," she said, "I can't back off. You are simply the most interesting thing going on here right now."

She seemed to be made of steel. For a moment I entertained the idea that she was a prostitute. But I didn't think that was likely—she wasn't getting down to business, she wasn't dressed appropriately, and she'd probably aged out of that occupation anyways.

No, she had to be a gold digger. A very obsessive one.

"Just back off," I ordered her. "I'm trying to make some coins to pay for my kids' school clothing."

That little lie should've been an instant turnoff. A man

who mentioned imaginary children should've killed any burgeoning tingles. But that didn't seem to register either.

I went back to playing, and she stayed parked right alongside me. I utterly ignored her, zeroing in on the cards. I won four hands in a row.

Then I doubled down and won big, four hundred bucks, on a sixteen hand to a dealer bust. The cougar whooped and threw her arms around my head and pulled my face into her chest. I couldn't breathe. It was like being smacked with a pair of medicine balls.

"What is your *name*?" she shouted. "I really *like* you."

That's when my patience broke. I couldn't handle this stalker who was too dumb to get my hints. Calling security wasn't an option either, since that was unwanted attention.

If I'd been there alone, I wouldn't have stuck around. But quitting wasn't an option. McCauley had made it clear that I needed to perform. The boys' college educations, not to mention my rent, were depending upon my performance. People needed me.

The cougar was relentless, though, following me to the next table. When she started giving me a head massage, I finally snapped.

I swept up my winnings, dumped them into my pocket, and headed across the floor to the cashier windows. Then I pushed through the front door and broke into a run, down the long walkway lined with red, white, and blue palm trees. I didn't look to see if the cougar was behind me. I didn't care.

It was back to the van.

THIRTY-FIVE

McCauley was standing outside the van, leaning against the hood. His nose looked especially reddened. Most of the boys had already returned.

I cleared my throat. "Four thousand six hundred dollars."

"That's it?"

"Yes."

He grabbed the envelope from my hands and handed it to Helen. She began counting. "That's all there is."

We were standing outside the van, the ten boys circled around us. McCauley fixed me with a dirty look.

Then he turned to Perry. "You, search him."

I realized now what he was suspecting: that I was skimming off the winnings. "I swear that's everything," I said. "It was a bad night."

But Perry was already crouched behind me, checking my pockets, patting down my legs. He was surprisingly good at it.

"Where did you learn how to do that?" I said.

"My dad's a cop."

The irony wasn't lost on me. Perry stood up. "He's fine, Father."

"It was a bad night," I said.

"Damn right it was, Jake. I give you three thousand dollars and ten professional-quality card counters, and you barely make fifty percent on my money."

"That'd be stellar in a mutual fund," I cracked.

"This isn't funny," he said. "These boys are depending on you."

"He stood up when the count was plus nine," said Samuel.

The priest turned apoplectic. "The count goes plus nine and De Niro here decides to leave the table? Colman, tell me that your partner's lying. I'm going to have a coronary right here if you don't."

Colman swallowed nervously. "No, it's true. Jake left the table on a plus nine."

McCauley went to punch the tree, then thought better and stopped. He whirled on me and pointed an accusatory finger. "That was your third strike, Jake. You're out. Off the team."

I felt a fury rising inside my torso. "What they're not telling you, Father, is that there was this woman who wouldn't leave me alone. She followed me *everywhere*. Every time I went to a new table, she was there, flirting, rubbing on me, pointing at the cards. I couldn't concentrate. She was being a total nuisance. Ask these kids. They all saw her."

"Is it true?" said McCauley.

"That's true," said Michael. "She was all over him."

That was nice, but McCauley still looked skeptical. "Did everybody see her?"

"She looked like a really slutty mom," confirmed Samuel.

McCauley looked at me with suspicion. "She wouldn't leave you alone?"

"With God as my witness," I said. "She was made of glue."

Suddenly McCauley looked stricken. "Wait a minute. Did she bring you any drinks?"

"Yes."

"Did she try to get your name?"

"Yes."

"And she pretended not to hear when you said to get lost?"

"Yes."

"And did she call you Jack?"

I thought back. "Yes, when she first approached me."

The old priest drew himself up to his full height. He was taller than everybody else anyways, so it was unnecessary. He looked like he was about to make an important pronouncement.

"That," he said, "was a *Hey Jack* girl."

Silence. Then Seth said, "Like a prostitute?"

The other boys snickered. They'd been thinking the same thing.

"No," said McCauley, "she's a professional distracter. We used to call them *Hey Jack* girls because that's what they said when they sidled up alongside you and didn't know your name."

I cleaned out my ear theatrically with my pinky. "Let me make sure I heard this right. That woman was being *paid*, by the casino, to *prevent* me from winning money."

"Yes. It's a wise investment when a player like you is winning two hundred dollars on each hand."

I laughed. "She was at least fifty years old."

"It's a Monday night," he said. "She was probably subbing for a younger girl. Get back in the van, boys, we've got to get you home by curfew."

As the kids filed into the van, McCauley took me by the shoulder and drew me away.

"I remember those girls," he said. "I've had to play over them before. It's not easy. I'm sorry. You can stay on the team."

He stuck his hand out. It was an honest apology. I shook it. "Thank you."

"But I'm still disappointed," he added.

"So am I."

"What can we do to make sure next time goes better?"

I thought about it. "I could have an entourage."

"What?"

"Not a big one," I explained. "Just a couple of people to stand on either side of me. They don't need to talk. I'll incorporate it into the act. Maybe a couple of girls."

McCauley stroked his chin. "A couple of girls, hm. Our next trip is to Temecula on Wednesday. Are you thinking what I'm thinking?"

I smiled. We would find out soon enough.

THIRTY-SIX

Three days later, I was back in that van again, staring at a mane of lustrous black hair. It had been washed, conditioned, sprayed, and lacquered within an inch of its life. I squinted hard. There was an extension visible.

The hair belonged to Thelma. Next to her was an identical black mane belonging to Velma. They were sitting on the first bench.

The rest of us were squeezed extra tightly to make up for it. Michael was sitting next to me. He was discreetly trying to lean forward and peer over their bare shoulders. I knew he wouldn't dare speak to them. He wasn't that bold.

But Seth was. He tapped Velma on the shoulder. "Excuse me, do you have a light?"

"Yeah," said Velma, reaching into her purse. The two women looked a little nervous. I wouldn't blame them. They were riding in a locked van with twelve teenage boys. Even skanks don't deserve that kind of treatment.

She handed him a lighter. "Here you go."

"Thank you," Seth said. He put it into his pocket.

Velma twisted around in her seat. "Aren't you going to use it?"

"No," he replied. The kid could barely contain his delight at speaking to such a gloriously sexy creature. "I just wanted to have one."

She sent him a nasty look. It couldn't penetrate his smirk. His face never wore anything else. I could see that he was the skeeziest of the ten boys—had the poorest impulse control, the darkest personality traits. You could depend upon him to take the easy way out in every situation.

I jumped into the conversation. "It was a good line, Seth," I said, "and executed well. But you should probably give her the lighter back."

"Aw, come on, Jakey," he said.

"There's no 'y' in my name. Give it back."

He reluctantly handed the lighter back to the girl. She snatched it back and turned around again.

Outside the window passed the rolling hills of Southern California. This was the no-man's land of eastern Orange County, where the scrub is baked yellower than straw half the year.

In the front seat, I saw McCauley clip a small head-phone into his ear. Then he jabbed a button on the console. Suddenly his voice came across the van's speakers.

"Can everybody hear me with this thing?" he said.

"That's so cool," said Michael.

"You'd better believe it," said the priest. "I don't have to twist this old carcass around to be heard any more. Now, one point of order. It's been brought to my attention that you've been texting each other on the floor. That is barred."

The boys cried out, but McCauley kept his cool. I could see how he'd commanded a classroom for decades.

"Use your brains, crybabies. Text messages are

evidence. This squad doesn't leave anything in writing. Besides, those bastards might have a text-message reading technology."

"That's insane," said Perry.

"Maybe, but here's a scenario that's not," the priest replied. "If they ever collar you, they might look inside your phone. If they see that you've been bragging about a running count of plus seven, how well do you think they'll treat you in that backroom?"

Perry lowered his head, humiliated. That was more plausible.

"Now, about tonight," said the priest. "Temecula is a busy casino, and it's Friday night. It's also the second of the month, which means we're going to have all the senior citizen buses."

"Why is that?" I said.

"Because they just got their Social Security checks. Now, what does this mean for you?"

"We have to stay cool," said Colman.

"Absolutely," answered the priest. "The old biddies are going to talk your ears off. Don't let them. Keep that count running. Second string, you guys are the buffer. Keep them away from the first string—but treat them with respect. Is that clear?"

In the rearview mirror, his eyes searched the van. The boys all nodded. These boys were disciplined. At their age, I'd been an acne-ridden, hormonal bag of self-conscious tics and twitches. Then again, I hadn't been offered a way to get a free college education.

McCauley continued: "Good. Table minimums are ten dollars again. I'm optimistic. If Jake learns how to avoid squealing like a scared little piggy again, we should make some decent money tonight."

I scowled at the priest but kept my mouth shut. There was no reason for him to bust my balls in front of everybody.

The van stopped. "We're here. You've got three hours."

"Three?" I said.

"Those old people are going to slow you down."

As the boys piled out of the van, they glanced at me, then at the girls. I detected more than a little jealousy.

"Should we get out too?" asked Velma.

"Not yet, sweetie," I said. "You're staying with me tonight."

THIRTY-SEVEN

Thirty minutes later, I was standing at the edge of the steps, surveying the blackjack tables below.

It was a sea of white hair. My nose twitched as the smell of rose hips wafted into my nostrils. I could almost see doilies spinning in front of my eyes.

McCauley, as usual, had been dead right. There'd been no less than fifty buses idling in a special parking lot behind the casino. Now, inside, we were seeing the disgorged contents.

Temecula Casino, at least for tonight, was the playground of the elderly.

I looked to my left. Thelma, standing inside the crook of my arm, smiled back at me. She was all tooth and gloss.

I looked to my right. Velma was tossing her hair and looking at passing men. She saw me looking at her.

"None of that tonight," I said. "You're with me. Besides, the casino has lots of girls like you on contract. And I'm sure they charge more."

Velma scowled. "Whatever."

"Your face is going to freeze like that. Now let's see

baby give her biggest smile."

She gave me an enormous fake smile. It was so brittle that I could've shattered it with a flick of my little finger.

This was going to be an easy role to play tonight—a high roller of the lowest order, a white boy wallowing in the mud. I'd dressed for the part in a cheap-ass shiny blue suit and nylon trucker cap. Helen had given me eighty bucks out of the slush fund to buy both. I'd even practiced my finger-gun winks. They'd be shooting around the casino soon enough.

"Ladies," I said, "are you ready to make some money?"

They tittered perfectly, knees knocking back and forth, their hair tossing. They'd had a lot of practice.

"We do need to talk about your only task," I said.

They looked at me vacantly. Maybe the word *task* had confused them. "Your job is to stand by me, just we are now, on either side of me. Cheer when I win. Console me when I lose. And whatever you do, don't let anyone bother me."

Thelma nodded. Velma did too. That was their most valuable skill set.

Slipping into character, I descended onto the gambling floor with immense swagger. The girls walked slightly behind me. I could hear their cheap bracelets jangling against one another. I nodded at anybody within eyesight. It felt like a movie scene.

In fact, I had played a scene like this, four years earlier. It'd been an indie movie about a bunch of young guys who wanted to make one last score in Vegas before getting out of gambling—until the mob discovers them. It had been unbelievably clichéd, but nobody ever went broke underestimating the public. Plus, it paid me scale, and that scale had paid my rent that month.

This wasn't fiction, though. In my pocket I was carrying three thousand dollars of chips. In my heart was the unsettling knowledge that I would be fired if I didn't knock this one out of the park.

Samuel signaled me with a stretch and four bounces to the left. It was a minus count. I decided to join him. Starting small would relieve the pressure for a while. I took the only remaining seat at the table and wagered two hundred smackers. Velma and Telma stood behind me with their hands on my shoulders.

The old lady next to me slid her ten-dollar chip across the felt. Then she glanced at Velma and Thelma. Her lip curled.

"What's the matter?" I said.

"No respectable man would dare be seen with these women in my day," she spat.

"Maybe," I said, "but this is all mine, at least until something better comes along."

"For you or for them?"

"Hey, I dropped out of school, grandma," I replied. "This is considered winning where I come from."

"You should know better," she said.

I looked up at Velma. "Hey, do your job."

Velma moved between me and the old woman. I concentrated on the cards. First, I got a sixteen against the dealer's jack. Even with the count so minus, I decided to hell with it and stood. The dealer busted.

My eyebrows lifted. I'd just won two hundred dollars on a minus four count. I wasn't supposed to be able to do that, at least not easily.

I decided to lose the next time, just for show, but the next hand went the same way. I got another sixteen, stood, and the dealer busted again. I won the third deal too.

The old lady peered around Velma. "You're doing something right," she said.

"It's all the estrogen," I replied.

On the outside, I was acting exuberant, but inside I was calculating things. The probability of winning three such hands was low. Maybe Colman had gotten the count wrong. Maybe he was setting me up.

I stayed on the table for another thirty minutes. I won thirteen hands, lost two, and pushed once. At the end, I scooped up my winnings. It was twenty-two hundred dollars.

"Lookee here," I bragged to the girls.

With giant smiles, Velma and Thelma kissed me on either cheek and slipped their arms around my waist. I noticed their pupils had dilated, so they weren't acting either. Something in them was predisposed to gravitate to winners.

Perry signaled me with five bounces to the right. I pointed my entourage towards his table and debouched onto an open seat like the Sun King descending from a carriage.

Over the next forty-five minutes, I won fifteen hands. I didn't lose one. Three thousand dollars in black chips grew in a pile before me.

"Congratulations," said the dealer when I finally stood up.

I flipped him a black chip and smirked. A skank on each arm, I swung around and moved through the tables. We were a low-rider, cruising slowly, nodding at passersby, drawing attention. I was deep into douchebag character now.

Most importantly, I looked stupid enough that nobody would ever suspect that we were associated with a team of card-counters.

Then I saw the pit boss heading towards me.

THIRTY-EIGHT

The pit boss was short, squat, and bald. He was swinging his left fist into his palm as he walked. You could see that he hadn't exactly been to the manor born. He could barely keep the monkey suit on.

"You're having a good night," he said.

"Hell yeah," I replied. "You stack the decks or something tonight?"

He ignored the joke. I would have too. "Here's some goodies for ya," he said, slipping something into my hand. It was a coupon for a free night's stay at the Temecula Casino Inn. They'd comped me a room.

"Thanks for the hookup, buddy," I said.

"You deserve it, pal. Say, what's your name?"

"Frankie," I lied.

"Frankie, would you be interested in signing up for our preferred customer list? It'll entitle you to all sorts of free discounts on your next visit."

McCauley had warned me about this. "You know," I said, "gambling is a real problem for me. I shouldn't even be here tonight."

The pit boss laughed. "That's a shame. You seem like somebody we'd like to welcome more often. Have a good night with your lovely ladies," he said, winking.

"Now we will," I said.

He shook my hand, then slunk away like a wolf that's just been denied a chance at a kill. I turned the girls and kept swaggering, but my stomach was secretly churning.

It'd finally happened. The pit bosses were watching me, and they'd given me a very indirect warning. It'd been inevitable, though, that I'd attract their attention sooner or later. McCauley had said that nothing stands out in a casino more than a scruffy young man playing for big money. And by playing that role, I kept the spotlight off the team of ten clean-cut young men playing for small money as they counted.

But it was nerve-racking nonetheless.

Colman signaled me that the count was plus seven. I started sweating. The pit bosses were onto me—and now here I was being invited to make another few thousand. I couldn't say no. I couldn't say yes.

Then I figured out the casino's strategy. I was the douchebag on a roll, and a free hotel room was their way of luring me off the gambling floor to enjoy the fleshy pleasures of my beskirted companions.

I stopped walking. Thelma and Velma looked at me with shining eyes. To them, every word out of my mouth was a pearl.

"Ladies," I said, "take this coupon and go over to the resort next door and check in. You can get the room ready for me."

I briefly lifted the coupon in the air, high enough to attract the pit bosses, and brought it down into the Velma's hand. Her eyes flashed but she didn't look surprised. She'd been waiting for this. She'd probably been through this wringer dozens of times. It wasn't classy, and it wasn't right, but this was her world.

"Sure," said Thelma.

"Oh *yes*," said Velma.

"But one of you has to wait in the lobby for me," I said. "And be discreet. Hide behind a plant or something. I'll be along in a little while."

I spun the skanks off my arm and slapped their jiggly asses. They squealed and minced off down the carpet, tossing their hair. I knew the pit bosses would be watching.

I exhaled. Now the pit bosses would hopefully stop dogging me, and I could make even more money.

I jammed a toothpick between my teeth and swaggered over to Colman's table. The old women recoiled from me as I approached. It was fun playing a douchebag.

It was even more fun winning four thousand dollars in the next half hour. I doubled down, split, hit hard and soft, even occasionally played wrong to lose a hand or two, to which I reacted theatrically.

An hour later, I'd finished the rounds of the tables. I'd lost count of how much I'd won. My pockets were literally bulging with black chips.

I looked up. The balding pit boss was whispering something into the ear of another man. He had narrow eyes and long snout of a wolf.

And the wolf-man was looking directly at me.

An itchy feeling radiated across my back. Every muscle fiber in my body stood up with a bullhorn and loudly announced that it was time to split.

As soon as the hand was over, I thanked the dealer, tipped him, swept the chips into my inside coat pocket, and walked towards the front lobby.

Moving through the tables, I had to stop myself from running. At the top of the staircase, the same one I'd descended earlier, I turned around.

The wolf-man was on the floor now, discreetly threading his way across the tables—and when he looked up, his narrow eyes were boring into my own.

THIRTY-NINE

Holy shit.

I turned and sprinted up the staircase, two at a time, clutching my coat so the chips wouldn't fall out. I was sure that an entire year's worth of college tuition was jangling in there.

Friday night at nine o'clock pm, and the lobby was swarming with hundreds of gamblers, partiers, and other people. That was the good news. The bad news is that I was dressed like a peacock. I ripped the nylon trucker hat off my head and tossed it into a garbage can. I was stuck with my shiny blue suit.

I couldn't go to the cashier. That would be inviting trouble. I'd have to leave the casino with the chips, and McCauley would have to send the team back in shifts to cash them in later. The priest had warned me about this, but it was a small price to pay.

I pushed through the doors and went out onto the sidewalk. It was possible to walk to the Temecula Inn without leaving the building—there was a carpeted hallway connecting it to the casino—but I was trying to lose the wolf-man.

Outside, I sprinted down the sidewalk, dodged left into a garden, ran through the bushes, hopped a hedge, threaded my way through a pair of dumpsters, slipped into a loading zone, and wandered the guts of the resort until I found the employees' door leading into the lobby.

I peeked around the edge. The space was sleek and modern. My eyes scanned the Japanese décor, the green bamboo planters, the sheet of water trickling down a four-story wall of black shiny slate. It made me want to don a kimono and hold a tea ceremony.

That would have wait. At this moment, I needed to find the skanks, and quickly I spotted Velma. She was sitting in a white leather chair with her naked legs crossed. Right in the middle of the lobby, for all the world to see.

I swore under my breath. It was my fault for asking someone who was hired for her outrageous body to act discreetly. I scanned the room for wolf-man. It wasn't inconceivable that he was going to accost me. After all, I was still technically on premises, pockets bulging with chips that should've been cashed in. But he wasn't anywhere to be seen.

I walked quickly across the open lobby to Velma. "What room did we get?"

She stuttered in response.

"What's the room number," I hissed. "Someone's after me."

"I forgot, wait, let me call—"

"Call her in the elevator." I grabbed her arm. Her skin felt sticky with dried sweat. I yanked her out of the chair and heard her stilettos on the hard floor behind me.

At the elevator, I jabbed the up button at least a dozen

times. It was an eternity and a day until one arrived. The doors opened and I bolted inside. Velma had the phone to her ear. "It's room six forty-seven," she said.

I pushed the close-door button. In the three seconds before the doors slid shut, I spotted wolf-man enter the lobby. His narrow-set eyes roamed the lobby like a predator —and fell upon me. I was helpless, framed inside an elevator.

He immediately started towards me. The doors closed and the elevator car began to rise.

"That was the guy," I said to Velma.

"Who?"

"Never mind. Listen, we have to get Thelma and leave right away. He's going to ask the front desk for our room number."

"Um—"

She looked nervous. "What?" I said.

"Nothing."

The doors opened on the sixth floor. I left the elevator and dashed down the hallway, the sconces and numbers flashing by. Velma was right behind me, doing that weird run that women do in high heels.

Then room 647 appeared on the left. I screeched to a halt. "Key."

"Let's knock first—" she said.

"Give me the key," I ordered.

She handed over the keycard. I slid it into the lock. The light turned green. I turned the lock and pushed inside.

It was a nice room. The décor was Swedish modern, clean lines and blonde wood and accent lights. I saw the bed on the far end of the room. On the bed was Thelma. She was reclining and sipping a flute of champagne.

She was also naked.

I stood there gaping. My lungs had seized up. I tried to speak, but my throat had dried out. It felt like I was having a coronary.

"Hi Jake," she cooed.

With great effort, I ripped my eyes from Thelma's hourglass figure. Then I faced Velma, who was standing alongside me. She was wearing a pink halter top. Something wicked in her eye told me she wanted that halter top peeled off.

Then it hit me. I was standing on the precipice of realizing one of the most desired fantasies of a man's sexual life.

I forced the thought out of my head. We needed to leave, pronto. The teenage boys were depending on these chips. And these girls probably had the latest and greatest in sexually transmitted diseases.

I became all business. "Get dressed," I ordered, pointing at the tiny pile of fabric on the floor. "We're going. *Now*."

Thelma sat up. She looked suddenly different. Minus the intergalactic slutwear, she looked different, like a pudgy Mexican girl with too much eye shadow and puffy brown nipples.

"So fast?" she said.

"I have a responsibility," I said. "Let's go. Or else you don't get paid."

That got her moving. In less than twenty seconds, Velma had suited up, and I was pushing both of them out of the door.

They headed back towards the elevator, but I whistled and nodded the other way. "We have to take the stairs. They're going to be coming up that way."

We found the staircase and began circling down the steps. The girls' heels made an awful racket that echoed up and down the concrete column.

We arrived in the main lobby. I crossed the floor quickly, the girls right behind me, feeling the stares of the front desk staff. They'd probably been told to watch for us. We didn't exactly blend in.

At the front door, my feet hit the motion-sensitive pad, and the automatic door flew open. The brisk night air felt good on my overheated face.

A bellhop tried to greet me, but I pushed my way past him. He would forgive me. I was, after all, doing God's work.

Five minutes later of heavy puffing later, we were two blocks off property, but I didn't slow my pace until we'd climbed back inside the van. I handed all the chips over to Helen and watched her count.

"What's the take?" I said.

In the front seat, Helen smiled at me in the rearview mirror. "Eleven thousand dollars, Jake."

The boys shouted, stamped their feet, clapped me on the shoulder. Helen turned to the priest. "Patrick, what do you think?

McCauley shrugged. "It's not bad."

That was the best compliment that I would get from him. But it didn't matter. I knew that I had earned my bones. I was officially a part of the team.

FORTY

From that moment on, the team fused together. It was like being strapped to the back of a Roman candle—with the old priest lighting the wick.

McCauley accelerated the schedule. We drove to two different casinos a week. Over the holidays, when the seniors were on winter break, we even took a ten-day trip, travelling to nine different casinos in the north of the state, from San Francisco up to Eureka.

Soon we'd run out of new casinos, and I suggested the obvious: Las Vegas. It was ground zero for gambling, and it was only five hours away. McCauley nixed the idea, however, explaining that such a gig would expose us to charges of transporting minors across state lines. Coming from a priest of questionable morality, that was understandable.

The pages continued flying off the calendar—days, weeks, months.

Listening to the boys' conversation, I began to absorb the ins and outs of counting, the pros and cons of the Omega 2 system.

During late-night drives, with the boys either asleep or deep into their earbuds, I would sometimes take the wheel of the van while McCauley explained things to me. He told me how, because of all the DIY materials out there, thousands of amateur counters tried to take the casinos every year. He described the typical profile of a counter—a young unkempt white male, looking harried, gambling alone, for big dollars. Look anything like him, and you will draw the wrath of the pit bosses. Most were spotted immediately. It was clear why McCauley controlled the boys' wardrobe, why he checked their hygiene, why they were coached to socialize, why they played in pairs.

Another thing he talked about a lot was the ladder of failure. Vegas, he said, was littered with degenerates, sloppy counters who'd first been barred from the one-deck games, then from the two- and three-deck games, then from the four- and five-deck games, and who were now relegated to playing nickel checks on six- and eight-deck games with shitty penetration. Guys who traded secret information about warped decks and incomplete shuffles.

He said that it was all garbage.

I guess I should say that *penetration* isn't a sexual word here. It refers to how deeply the dealer dives into the shoe. The friendlier the dealer, the deeper the penetration—and the higher the count.

Then the priest told me about the dark art of dealer tells. About how dealers sometimes will lift up the corner of an ace twice, because the tip of an A resembles the tip of a 4.

I also learned how he picked the casinos. It was a phone app, updated daily with information about which casinos were offering which types of games. He said that the single-

or double-deck games drew amateur counters like flies on the weekends. Since we were using team play, we wouldn't need those games anyways, and thus we avoided them.

Then there was the matter of the flask. He always kept discreetly tucked between his foot and the console. Sometimes, when it was very dark and quiet in the van, he would bend over, pretending to search for something, and drain the flask completely. It seemed sketchy, but it wasn't my place to say anything.

Finally, after three straight months of betting, McCauley gave the team a week off. It was the second week of January, and the boys had final exams.

I took the opportunity to go surfing. It's my passion, my happy place. On this day, the waves were barely four feet high, and they were breaking clean too, so I couldn't get any speed up. Plus the air temperature was a crisp fifty-five degrees. I gave up after an hour and carried my board back to my apartment.

Standing in my living room, I peeled off my dripping neoprene wetsuit—and saw the the voicemail icon on my phone. I played the message.

It was McCauley. "Sorry to disturb your vacation, Jake, but the team has an urgent assignment. Stop by tonight at six pm please. I have your commission for the last two weeks as well."

His phrasing was interesting. It sounded as though some governing body were forcing him to make this call.

I scowled. I'd been hoping, for just one night, to wrap myself in a bathrobe and sit down with a good old-fashioned mystery novel. It's always novels for me because I can't watch television. After you've seen how the pigs are slaughtered, the last thing you want to do is fry some bacon.

But bathrobe night wasn't going to happen. This team had me travelling more than an archaeologist. And no matter how chummy we had become, I couldn't forget that McCauley still had my nuts in a sling.

Still, tonight, he was going to pay me. I sighed and began to get dressed.

FORTY-ONE

Xavier High School was situated in an old neighborhood of Los Angeles that had once been occupied by Greek immigrants. Not much of their culture was left except the delicious smell of lamb and spanakopita wafting out of Papa Cristo's, a nearby eatery.

It was a local landmark and one of my favorite places. I parked my car and went inside and devoured a grilled octopus with rosemary roasted potatoes. I washed it down with a Styrofoam cup of strong red wine.

Then I drove on to the high school.

Xavier was a four-story structure with a red Spanish tiled roof. This time of night, it was a looming dark presence behind heavy gates. I parked on the street and slipped in through the pedestrian entrance. The grounds were empty, except for a soccer team leaving the field. The lights on the practice field clicked off.

Now, save for a lonely streetlamp, the grounds were almost totally dark. I pulled the coat against my chin and moved quietly across the campus. At last I found the Jesuit

Residence. It was a three-story edifice nestled against the side of the high school.

I approached the heavy front door. It was wooden and coffered. My finger pressed the doorbell. I felt disembodied, separate from myself. I'd probably been gambling too much. It has that effect on you.

A slim, middle-aged man opened the door. A pair of sturdy little scholarly glasses was perched on his nose. He was wearing the red sweater and black shirt and black pants ensemble that Father McCauley favored. These must be the Jesuit duds of choice.

"Yes?" he said.

"I'm here to see Father McCauley," I said.

"Regarding?"

My eyes flitted around while I tried to think of a good lie. "The new coaching position. On the hockey team."

"Oh," he said, "I wasn't aware that there was a new coaching position available on the hockey team. Or that Father McCauley was affiliated with the hockey team." He scratched his temple thoughtfully. "Come to think of it, I didn't even know that we had a hockey team."

"Somebody in the administration must know."

"I'm assistant principal."

I felt my cheeks blush. "It's only in the planning stages. You'll hear about it soon."

"Of course." The smile on the Jesuit's face told me that he knew exactly why I was there. "Have we spoken before?"

That was when I recognized his voice. It was thin, reedy, professorial—the same voice that had promised to leave a message for McCauley months earlier.

"I don't know," I said. "Have you worked as a second assistant director on any television series recently?"

It was a weird answer. The man looked at me as though

I'd just descended a stepladder from an alien spacecraft. "Tell you what—why don't you just come this way. I think Patrick is in the library."

I followed him into the residence. It felt like a sixteenth-century monastery. The floors were dark brown tiles, polished to a bright shine. Black iron chandeliers hung overhead. I imagined all sort of Counter-Reformation torture devices in the cellar, Torquemada wickedly rubbing his hands together, but that was just my overactive imagination.

"I'm Father James," he said. We were ascending a circular staircase. The railing felt cold underneath my right palm. "The architect was aiming for something with a classic feel."

I peered down the staircase. "I'm feeling Wuthering Heights."

At the top was another coffered wooden door. The Jesuits loved them. Father James opened it, then stepped aside, gesturing for me to enter. I obeyed.

I stepped into the Jesuits' private library—cordoban leather chairs, old globes, rows of leatherbound books. The kind of place I wouldn't mind getting lost in for a few hours.

In the middle of the room sat Father McCauley.

FORTY-TWO

The old priest was in an overstuffed leather chair. His legs were crossed over the knee. His eyes were staring at the opposite wall and his lips were moving silently. I watched his fingers tap an intricate rhythm on the armrest. This is what it looked like when someone much smarter than I am pondered higher mathematics.

"Patrick," said the priest, "you have a visitor."

McCauley jerked out of his trance. "Ah, Jake, you made it. The lure of money."

"I would've crawled here on my hands and knees."

"How very Catholic. You met Father James?"

"I did."

"Would you like something to drink?"

The words were barely out of his mouth when Father James fixed him with a curious stare. Even I felt uncomfortable. McCauley must've felt it too, but he didn't flinch. His hide was as tough as an alligator's.

"You know what I like," I said.

"Scotch," the old priest said, looking at James. "In fact, make it a double. He's one of the good ones."

Father James went over to a liquor cabinet and unlocked it using a key from a chain around his neck. He withdrew a bottle of Dewar's and poured a healthy slug into a crystal lowball glass, then recapped the bottle and replaced it inside the cabinet and closed the door and locked it again. Then he stuffed the key back underneath his sweater and brought the glass over to me.

"That's a lot of security for a drink," I said. "Did it kill somebody?"

"Not yet," Father James said, glancing at the old priest.

McCauley ignored him. "I have a couple things to show you, Jake. First, I did a breakdown of the fall semester season."

He stopped talking. He'd seen the alarmed look on my face.

"What it is?" he said.

"Shouldn't we be alone?" I replied, inclining my head towards the other priest. The scholarly Father James had taken a seat at a nearby desk, positioned a reading light, and begun poring over a heavy leatherbound book.

"Him?" said McCauley. "Oh, he knows about the team."

"Really."

McCauley grinned. "I'd say so—considering that he funds it."

I wanted to keep a straight face. Of course, I also wanted to cut down on carbohydrates before bedtime. I couldn't do that either.

I turned to Father James. "Is that true?"

He didn't bother looking up from the book. "I save my little pennies all year long."

"Father James provides seed money each year," said

McCauley. "It comes out of his own personalia. That's our monthly stipend."

"And I'm not the only one," added James.

"We all contribute here," said McCauley. The old Jesuit donned a pair of reading glasses and produced a black folder from his attaché case. It was a tablet. I don't know why it surprised me to see priests using new technology.

He tapped on the screen and brought up a spreadsheet. "My goal," he said, "is perfect team play. If achieved, it results in a two percent win rate. Here, look at this equation."

He pointed at the screen. It said $W = (B)(E)(T)$.

"What does that mean?"

"Hourly win rate equals average bet times percent advantage times hands per hour."

I felt my eyes glaze over. "So what are we at?"

"One point seven percent. That's very, very good. In fact, we're already at five hundred thousand dollars."

That was impressive. It was halfway through the school year, and we were only two hundred thousand short. At this rate, the boys would reach the goal in six weeks.

"That's good," I said. "Have you had a two percent year yet?"

"Nineteen ninety-five."

Father James cut in. "And he *never* stops talking about it."

A nostalgic smile appeared on McCauley's face. "God, those boys were professionals," he said. "A vintage year. Like a port that you just can't stop sipping." His fingers swirled an imaginary glass.

"Easy, friend," said James.

A look of irritation flashed across the old man's eyes, then he regained himself. "Okay, Jake, down to business. I owe you some money. Four percent of the last month's winnings."

He handed me a thick envelope. I peeked inside. It was a stack of fifty-dollar bills.

"How much is it?"

"A little over four grand."

I sat back, nodding. This wasn't the reaction he was looking for. "Go on," he said, "jump for joy. Act greedy. Get venal."

"If all I wanted was money," I said, "I would've gone into dry cleaning."

"How selfless."

I stowed the envelope in my coat pocket. "Do you ever feel guilty, Father McCauley?"

His face dropped. "About what?"

"About being both a priest and a card-counter at the same time."

Father James suddenly cleared his throat, set down his book, and turned in his chair. "Jake, our order has always worked illicitly."

"That's right," said McCauley.

Father James leaned forward in his chair. He used his index finger to push his glasses further up his nose. I figured this was his way of announcing that he was about to dominate the conversation.

"The Jesuit Edmund Campion," he said, "secretly ministered to sixteenth-century English Catholics while enduring persecution under the crown. In the seventeenth century, Matteo Ricci lived and dressed as a Mandarin to gain entry to the imperial Chinese court. John Corridan worked for labor reform in New York in the 1940s."

"You ever see *On the Waterfront*?" said McCauley.

That was one of my favorite movies. "Let me guess," I said. "The priest, played by Karl Malden."

McCauley nodded. "They based it on Corridan."

"And then we had Daniel Berrigan in the sixties, protesting the war in Vietnam," added James.

"That hotheaded mick," said McCauley, shaking his head. "Never met a brawl he couldn't brag his way into."

"And then Ignatius Loyola himself. The founder of our order. He built a house for reformed prostitutes—"

"The Santa Marta," finished McCauley. "I'm happy to say, Jake, that I am the latest in a very long line of Jesuits willing to get their hands dirty to achieve social justice. Any more dumb questions?"

He smiled sweetly at me.

I had nothing to say. McCauley was comfortable living in a paradox. His life existed at the intersection of the sacred and the profane.

"So what's the other thing you want to give me?" I said.

"This," said McCauley.

FORTY-THREE

He reached into his attaché case and pulled out a cheap black fanny pack with neon pink piping. It cost about two dollars and was the kind of thing a child would wear.

"Open it," he said.

I did so. Inside was even more money. I thumbed through the denominations. They were all clean hundred-dollar bills. I doubted that these had ever seen in the inside of a casino. They looked like they'd just been withdrawn from a bank.

"What's this?" I said.

"Count it out."

I removed the cash and began to count. My eyes grew wider as I passed five thousand. When I hit ten thousand, I stopped. "Can you just tell me?"

"Twenty-five thousand dollars."

I felt myself gag. "Why are you giving me this? I didn't earn this. I can't even *spend* this much."

The old priest shook his head. "I don't want you to keep it or spend it. I want you to *lose* it. At the tables. By yourself."

I was confused. The point of me sweeping through the boys' tables at every casino and putting down big bets on each one—even the losing tables, for slightly lesser dollars—was to lose the scrutiny of the pit bosses.

I grew impatient. "But I don't understand why you—"

"Because in past years," he said, interrupting, "our sweepers have encountered some resistance at this point."

"What do you mean, *resistance*?"

He looked sad. "See, Jake, we've run out of in-state casinos. We've visited all twenty-seven. Now we have to start repeating. And after your second big night in the same place, it's possible that you'll get collared. It's happened before."

"The other sweepers got barred?"

He nodded. "Some of them. I don't want the same to happen to you."

I didn't know whether to thank him or punch him.

"You must know how this hustle works by now," he said. "It's two steps forward, one step back. This is the one step back. And it's entirely voluntary." McCauley caught my eyes. "We'll still come out on top, though."

"The arc of the universe is long," added Father James, "but it bends towards justice."

It looked as though I didn't have a choice. There was nothing to really protest. "So which casinos do I go to?"

"These."

McCauley handed me a handwritten list. I read it closely. There were nine of them. He'd listed out the schedule, driving times, mileage, everything. I massaged my forehead. I would be puttering around California all week.

"This is a lot of driving," I said.

"Don't look so upset. I gave you five hundred extra for gas and hotel. Bring a girlfriend, make a vacation out of it.

Just be sure to publicly lose that money. Near the pit bosses, whenever possible. And only in the evenings."

"I'm surprised that you trust me with it," I said.

The old Jesuit fixed me with a crusty look. "Who says that I do?"

I thought back to the pictures that he'd blackmailed me with. Father James, meanwhile, was watching me with a curious smile. I suddenly felt an odd throbbing behind my eyes. These men were too smart, too manipulative. I needed to get out of that room.

"You're the boss," I said. Then I stood up and turned to Father James. "It's been nice meeting you."

I turned and left the room, descending the circular staircase. I couldn't get across the glossy brown floors, away from the iron candelabras, and out of this den of powerful gamblers, quickly enough.

But I also couldn't stop thinking about McCauley's last comment. *He didn't trust me.*

I was still thinking about that as I drove back across town towards my apartment, with the fanny pack fixed around my waist.

It was going to be a long week.

FORTY-FOUR

I wanted to rip the little black bowtie off the dealer. I'd been staring at it for the last hour and a half.

It'd become a symbol of all the money I was losing.

This was the fourth day of my odyssey to lose as much money gambling in the state of California as possible. And it was working. So far tonight, I'd lost nearly two-thirds of the hands I'd been dealt, to the tune of two thousand dollars. Over the last four days, I'd lost at least ten thousand dollars. I wasn't even bothering to track the stuff too closely. It didn't matter.

What mattered was McCauley's team of teenage counters. I missed them. The reason was obvious: I was a winner with them. Every neuron in my body cried out for those glorious stretches, those bounces, the dopamine fix that each win had squirted into my veins. The boys' knowledge of the running count was truly a crutch. Without them, I'd become just like every other sad sack gambler out there.

Even though it hadn't been my own cash, the losses had plunged my mood into the basement. There was a good doctoral dissertation for a psychologist somewhere in this.

I scowled at the bowtie again. The dealer was smirking. They weren't supposed to do that.

"Not your night," said the guy next to me.

He sounded friendly, but I was in a foul mood. "Shut up," I said.

"You shut up," he answered. "I'm just trying to be nice."

I twisted and looked at him. Normally I'm more liberal in my assessment of people but this was that kind of murderous mood. The guy looked like a pile of oozing, pustulous white flesh inside a rayon polo shirt. His lips were fastened around a plastic straw that led into a piña colada.

"Say that again?" I said.

"I said that your attitude isn't helping your cause any."

"That coconut milk isn't helping your BMI any either."

"Come on," he said, "we all have to learn how to lose."

"We also have to learn how to call a dermatologist."

"You could just leave, you know."

He was right. I snarled and shoved another two hundred out of my pocket onto the table. I glanced at the pit boss. He was smirking at me.

Deep inside my vicious mood, I congratulated myself on a mission nearly accomplished.

Then my phone rang. I looked at the display. It read Xavier High School. That was McCauley's number.

I picked up. "Loser central. You got a casino chip, I'll lose it for you, no questions asked."

"Jake," said a reedy, scholarly voice.

That wasn't McCauley. "Father James?" I said.

"Stop betting," he said. "Right now."

I had so much attitude in my belly that it was giving me indigestion. "I sincerely hope you're not going to blackmail me. Because I can only handle getting blackmailed by one priest at a time. Otherwise I get confused."

He wasn't in the mood either. "This isn't the time for joking. How much have you lost?"

I looked at the dealer. He was listening, and I didn't want to reveal my mission. "Almost half. It's been crushing to my spirit." Then I added bitterly, "Amen."

"Jake, I need you to stop gambling immediately and drive back to Los Angeles."

"Why?"

"I'll explain everything when you get here. Trust me."

He ended the call. I looked at the phone in my hand. Then I looked up at the dealer, at the other players. They were all looking at me.

"Sir?" said the dealer.

"I'm think I'm finished."

The fatty neighbor smiled. "The old lady doesn't like you throwing away the retirement money, huh."

I placed my hand on the fatty's shoulder. It startled him. He sloshed piña colada onto his shirt.

"I'm sorry," I said.

"For being yourself?"

"No, I'm not usually this much of a bastard. But I got some people yankin' my chain real hard."

"Then yank back."

"I wish I could," I said. I tossed a black chip into his cocktail, stood up from the table, and walked out.

FORTY-FIVE

On the freeway, I pointed the front of my car towards Los Angeles and set the cruise control. Every twenty minutes, I tried calling McCauley's mobile phone. He never picked up. I didn't leave him any message either. There was no point. Old priests aren't flaky. They, of all people, know the value of communication. If McCauley wasn't answering his phone, it was because he didn't want to talk.

On the other hand, if Father James had called me, something serious must've happened. I was guessing a heart attack.

Four hours later, I pulled into Xavier High School's parking lot. School was just letting out for the day. Hundreds of teenage boys in khakis and penny loafers were pouring out into the parking lot. I remembered that it was finals week. Some punched and pushed playfully, like young bucks. Others trudged slowly, heads down.

I swam through the school of adolescent fish and trekked up the front staircase into the lobby of the school. The school office was to my left. I stepped inside.

Behind a counter, a middle-aged woman was conferring

with a young boy, probably a freshman, who was crying. A golden brooch was pinned to her chest. It was shaped like Jesus pinned to a crucifix, head hanging down.

"That's terrible," she was saying. I tagged her as the school's *de facto* motherly figure. Every all-boys' high school needed one.

The kid was sniveling: "Can... can... I ... get ... an extension—"

"No," she replied nicely, "but there's nothing to worry about. You'll just have to take summer school classes."

He kept blubbering.

"Malcolm, look at me," she said. Then her index finger pointed towards the brooch on her chest. "You see this man? He had a real problem. You, on the other hand, failed algebra. You'll survive."

The kid ran past me, tears and snot sliding down his face. I tried not to smile and stepped forward.

The secretary greeted me with the same friendly professionalism. "Yes, sir, how can I help you?"

"I'm Jake," I said, "and I'm here to talk to Father James."

Her eyes tracked me up and down. I carried the stench of a losing gambler. It didn't seem to bother her. After all, she worked with teenagers. She was accustomed to stench.

"Can I tell him what this is regarding, Jake?"

"The janitorial position that's available. I believe it's called a sweeper."

I put extra sauce on that last word. She looked at me as though I had dyed my hair bright green and sprayed it straight up.

"I haven't heard of that position. Are you sure that you're at—"

"Just tell him," I said. "He'll understand."

Shrugging, she turned and headed into a back office

marked *Father Jim James*. I thought about that name for a minute. His parents must've been the least imaginative people on earth.

The lady reemerged a few seconds later, a knowing smile on her face. "Come on back, Jake."

I went around the counter and into the back office. Father James was standing there, waiting, a dark cloud massed over his head. He seemed somehow taller now, here in his office. It could be the perception of importance that he carried as vice principal of six hundred boys.

The priest closed the door but remained standing. I stayed standing too. That was fine with me. I'd been sitting for four days—in my car, at the blackjack tables, in my soul.

"McCauley is missing," he said flatly.

"Since when?"

"Thirty-six hours. We can't find him. He took one of our cars and fled."

"Why would he do that?"

Father James looked doubly grim and skipped the question. "This isn't the first time he's done this, Jake. It happened about fifteen years ago."

"Where did he go then?"

"Reno. The hotel manager called us. A housekeeper found him unconscious on the bathroom floor. I went to pick him up."

Something was missing from this story. I think I knew what it was.

"He's on a bender," I said.

The priest deflated slightly. He didn't bother to bluff this time. "Yes."

"So McCauley's an alcoholic."

"Recovering."

"Not really," I said. "He carries a flask in the van. And we met at a bar one night."

Father James turned away. He ruffled the hair on the back of his head. I guess that this was both surprising and unsurprising. "We've all tried to keep him on the straight and narrow. But he's got a monster of an addiction inside of him."

He paused, thinking. "The worst part," he finally said, "is that Patrick's *status* is going to be announced next month."

He pronounced that word in the Latin way, like sta-*toos*. I suspected it didn't mean what I thought. "What's that?" I said.

"It's his new assignment. And the Jesuit superior has been fed up with his shenanigans for quite some time." He paused. "I think Patrick's going to be sent to Manresa."

"What's that?"

"Our retirement home."

That was novel. I hadn't had any idea what happened when priests got too old to work. I'd assumed they prayed until age seventy, then were processed into communion wafers.

Then the real consequence of the news walloped me on the side of the head. If McCauley were put out to pasture, that would mean the end of the card-counting team. And we were only halfway through the school year.

Father James fell into a chair and looked at me. He seemed to be reading my mind. "The team's had a good run. Twenty-five years, right? I honestly can't believe Patrick carried it this long without getting busted."

Then my thoughts went to Michael. He was on the second string. He was only getting half his college tuition covered anyways. If the team collapsed now, he would probably only get half of the half, if even that much. Without further winnings to fill the pot, the compound interest on the investments would decrease, and the tuition payments would dry up.

His mother would be devastated.

"We can't let it collapse," I said. "I mean, there are so many people depending on this team. Plus, we have another trip scheduled for Saturday."

Father James shrugged. "It's up to you. Do what you want. I'll be in touch as soon as we find him."

We shook hands, and I exited the office and left the high school, feeling dazed. The future of this card-counting team was in my hands.

FORTY-SIX

In 1945, Harry Truman had only been vice-president for four months when his boss, President Franklin Delano Roosevelt, died. In the blink of an eye, Truman was pushed into the reins of power.

That was me.

I decided to preserve this team. Since the old priest hadn't returned my messages, I called each of the ten boys the next day and delivered the bad news—that Father McCauley was missing, but that the team would continue travelling to casinos for the time being. And that I was now the leader.

There was nobody else. Only Helen, but she had a stressful full-time job in finance. She had neither the hours nor the interest. The choice was clear: Either I took the reins, or it collapsed—and failure wasn't an option.

Plus I still had fifteen thousand dollars that I'd been asked to lose. It would've been ridiculously easy to abscond with it. I could've buried it in the sand along the Oregon coast. I could've flown to Fiji. I could've given it to some street kids on the curb outside.

But I couldn't have lived with my conscience. Mine is stronger than a Russian grandmother. That was going to be seed money for our next gambling trip.

We were scheduled to hit the Santa Ynez Casino on Saturday. I realized that we would need to find another fourteen-passenger van, since McCauley had always taken care of the rental. Fortunately, I had read McCauley's papers, and remembered that it'd been loaned from a Hertz office in the San Fernando Valley.

I drove up the 405 and over the hill and exited at Ventura Boulevard at the bottom of the hill. I found the office, a forgettable one-room outlet in a nowhere office plaza in Encino.

There was a fat woman at the front desk. A trash can full of empty yogurt containers told me that she had good intentions about that.

"I'm picking up a van," I said. "Fourteen passengers."

She tapped her pen against her teeth and scowled. "Of course you are."

We sat there, mentally circling one another like a couple of hyenas. "Are you going to help me," I said, "or are we just going to snort at each other all day?"

"What's the name on the reservation?"

"McCauley."

Her scowl deepened. "Unless you lost fifty years and a face full of wrinkles, you're a liar."

It was my turn to frown. I should've known that she would remember McCauley. He'd been renting this van twice a week for months, even years, now. "I'm picking up for him," I said.

"Did he finally get a DUI?"

"I don't know."

"Well, he's got to pick up in person," she replied.

"You can trust me. He'll return it. He's a man of the cloth."

She shot me skeptical look. "Have McCauley call us."

"I can't. He's sick this morning."

"Wake him up."

"It's a sleeping sickness."

"Jesus," she said, "you really don't get it."

"No, I get it. I just don't like taking it. Not from you."

I laid a twenty-dollar bill onto her desk. She looked up at me with a fiendish look on her face. "I bet you got another one of those. I know where you guys go in the van."

I slapped another twenty down. She nodded, then began to typing at her computer. "Father McCauley, can I have a copy of your C-class license, please?"

I didn't have that, so I laid down another twenty. She pulled that down into her purse. "On file already, excellent."

We went through the usual shenanigans. She'd extracted a hundred bucks from me by the time the keys were in my hand. I was lucky to have escaped with my shirt.

As I nosed the heavy van out of the parking lot, I wondered if Harry Truman had needed to grease the skids to get what he needed.

FORTY-SEVEN

The minute Colman started puking into his own baseball cap, I knew it was going to be a bad trip.

We were on Highway 246, two hours north of Los Angeles, heading up into the mountains above Santa Barbara. The two-lane road was a wickedly sinuous stretch of asphalt, a series of hairpin curves, passing lanes, and truck traffic.

Helen sat clutching the wheel of the fourteen-passenger van, sending it careening around the curves. Behind us, the ten boys were groaning as they slid into one another, left, then right, then left, then right.

I was in the passenger seat, clutching the oh-shit bar. "You've driven this before?" I said.

"Just once," she said.

"I think you're scaring the boys."

"They're young," she replied. "And I want to get home before midnight."

As the road straightened out, we began a long, gradual descent into the Santa Ynez Valley. I'd heard about this area, two and half hours north of Los Angeles, a valley where cows ran free half the year, where nearly everybody was a millionaire, where wineries had sprouted up like mushrooms after a rain. It was the place where you could see a guy in a cowboy hat pull up in a Lamborghini to his miniature horse ranch.

"I want to retire here," said Helen. "It's gorgeous."

"You don't have this type of money."

She shrugged. "A girl can dream." She yawned and stretched. "We'll be at the casino in about fifteen minutes. Time to rally the troops."

I cleared my throat and turned around. Ten pairs of adolescent eyes stared back at me. None looked particularly friendly. Seth looked outright hostile. I felt my stomach flip up like a wounded fish. I tackled it and brought it back down.

"Okay guys," I said, "since Father McCauley is taking a few days off—"

"Hungover," said Colman.

"With hookers," added Seth.

The boys all snickered. Truth be told, I would've made the same cracks, but my role as authority figure prohibited it. I began to pass out several envelopes. "Here's tonight's stake. The important thing is that nothing changes. We work in the same pairs as before. Again, nothing changes. Got it?"

Seth piped up. "When can we start to lay our own bets?"

"You can't," I said. "Steaming only. Hear me?"

"Yeah, whatever," he said. Something about his tone caught my ear. It carried the undertones of resistance, of antipathy, of anger.

"Ten to twenty dollars only," I repeated, fixing Seth with my best evil glance. "Hear me?"

"Loud and clear," he replied. But his eyes were looking elsewhere.

The van was speeding through the vineyards now, the parallel rows of brown winter vines zipping past the windows. I gazed at the signs advertising wine-tasting, 10 am to 5 pm, and regretted being in a van full of minors, even ones with fake IDs.

We had landed on the floor of the valley, and around a blind curve suddenly appeared the Santa Ynez Casino. Helen ignored the men in florescent orange vests on the side of the road trying to wave us into the parking structure.

As the road wore on, however, a different problem presented itself. There was no place to stop and park.

"These cowpoke towns," I said.

"Urban casinos are easier to approach," agreed Helen.

Three miles later, we came upon a small downtown area. Porky tourist families waddled around with ice cream cones. A sign said *Welcome to Solvang—Danish Country!* Helen pulled into a parking spot.

"We're stopping here?" said Perry. "Seriously? The casino was way back there."

"I told you to wear comfortable shoes," Helen said.

"What the hell," muttered Samuel.

"It's better than blowing the cover," I said. "We have no other choices. Look, you can cut across that field. That'll take off two miles of winding road."

I pointed across a vineyard. The top of the casino's roof was clearly visible over the vines, about a ten-minute walk away.

"But I'm wearing my Ferragamos," said Colman.

"Do you really want to incur six digits of college debt?" she answered.

"What's 'incur' mean?"

"It means get out," she replied. "All of you, let's make some money."

Grumbling, the boys stepped out of the van, two by two, as though disembarking from Noah's ark. I watched them trudge across the vineyard. When the last pair had disappeared, Helen turned to me.

"Jake, before you go, I have to tell you something."

"What?"

"This casino is different from the others."

"How?"

"From what I understand, the pit bosses here are particularly ... strict."

"Meaning observant," I said.

She nodded. "Meaning, don't break any rules."

I hated socializing with pit bosses. I'd already been approached a handful of times over the last three months. First came their presence at my side, then came the fake compliments, then the advice that always lay just on this side of insinuation. And I'd taken the advice, smiling all the way.

"Thank you," I said.

"Be careful. Call me if you have any problems."

As I closed the passenger door and set out towards the casino, I prayed that that wouldn't ever happen.

FORTY-EIGHT

The sun was beginning to fall in the sky, and I swiftly picked my way across the vineyard, through the bare vines. Underfoot, the dirt was dry and tamped down, owing to the lack of rain. I thanked God for small miracles.

Nearby, to the right, lay the tasting room of a stylish winery. On the outside patio were several modern firepits. I could see fashionable people gathered around them, their glasses of red wine reflecting the orange flames.

I managed to swallow my bitterness, but I couldn't stop thinking about my life. How it would've turned out differently if I'd finished college, if I hadn't become an actor. I probably could've been at that winery right now, wearing a turtleneck, sipping a meritage, my arm around the waist of a sophisticated woman, talking about the difficulty of finding health care for my fifteen hundred employees.

Instead, I'd become an unemployed, unmarriageable actor who was helping teenagers gamble. This was my life right now. I'd made these choices.

At the end of the vines, I climbed back up to the short embankment and walked the remaining quarter mile along the road until I came to the casino entrance. The security guy in the orange florescent vest glanced at me. His arms still waved the sticks at traffic. "You didn't have to park in Solvang," he said. "Lots of free spaces here."

"We ran out of gas," I lied.

"That's tough," he said. "You got ID?"

"Yeah, why?"

"Just checking."

I showed him my driver's license. He nodded and handed it back to me. "Enjoy your evening."

I walked past him, sweating a little. No other casino personnel had ever checked my identification before. And if he'd checked me, then he'd certainly checked the boys too.

This wasn't good.

The entrance to the casino could only be accessed from the parking structure, so I entered the ground floor and joined a flood of people pouring out of an elevator. We were escorted down a long green outdoor carpet, beneath a covered canopy, to the front of the casino.

Inside, several tubes of red, green, and blue florescent lights formed a chandelier over the entrance lobby. It felt the designer had been trying to envision a future of pure tackiness. A pair of semi-spiral staircases broke around a waterfall and led up to the gaming floor.

I inhaled deeply. It was the usual stink of nicotine and despair.

I trudged over to the cashier and cashed in three thousand dollars. She eyed me warily. I ignored the eye and stuffed my chips into my pockets and walked upstairs. It had begun feeling like a routine.

With time to kill before the counts became clear, I wandered through the casino, bored, glancing into places. I looked into a small ballroom where a couple hundred senior citizens were hunched over long tables, playing feeble games of bingo. I shook my head sadly. That wasn't how I wanted to end my life.

Next door, I peeked into a playroom full of wild-eyed toddlers beating each other with toys. The irony was ridiculous. You couldn't get child care at most major companies to help you make money—but it was right there, free of charge, at a casino, to help you lose money.

My foul mood was back.

I found the blackjack tables and immediately sensed something. A certain presence. I'd been in enough casinos now, had enough data points, to feel it. The forty or so tables had been circled together like a wagon train, and inside the circle stood several pit bosses. They huddled in a group, all staring in different directions, at different tables. They looked like a gang of predatory animals.

Christ. I'd never seen them on point like this. I started to sweat. If I started winning big, these bosses were going to give me the bum's rush.

Just then, Seth stretched and twisted three times to the right. I ignored him and went to an uncounted table near the pit bosses. I lost a few hands on twenty-dollar bets, just as a precaution. I could see Seth looking my way, trying to get my attention.

Then my phone beeped. I looked down. He'd just texted me. +4.

Annoyed, I stuffed my phone back into my pocket. True, the count was climbing, but I wondered what part of McCauley's instruction "nothing in writing" Seth didn't understand.

I lost a few more hands at my table. Then, suitably dejected, I strolled over to Seth's table and sat down.

"Hopefully you'll be nicer to me than he was," I said to

the dealer, jerking my thumb back towards the first table. The dealer said nothing. She was a large woman with long black hair and high almond eyes. Then I remembered that this was a Native American casino.

I glanced casually at Seth. He was drinking a glass of brown liquid flecked with white foam. It was a beer. I felt myself getting angry. He knew damn well that was forbidden. He also knew that with McCauley out, there was nobody to enforce his dismissal.

It made me angry. He was thumbing me in the eye, letting me know that I carried no weight whatsoever on this team.

I swallowed my anger and laid down a black chip. Another player whistled. Apparently nobody had been betting big on this table. The dealer handed me a four and a seven against her nine. That was a no-brainer. I told her to hit. It was a king, for twenty-one. The dealer busted. She shoved another black chip at me.

I let both chips lay. "Let's do two hundred this time."

She nodded and dealt again. This time, I got a jack and a three. "Stand," I said.

"On thirteen?" said the dealer.

I nodded. The count was too high. There were too many face cards in the shoe. I was sure to bust.

Sure enough, the other players busted. The dealer busted. She shoved me two more black chips.

Five minutes ago, I had laid down a hundred dollars. I now had four hundred.

"What the hell?" said Seth. He was looking at me. "This guy sits down here and cleans up."

My stomach flipped. First he ordered a beer. Now this kid was explicitly breaking another team law—don't acknowledge teammates. And don't draw unnecessary attention to my freakish winnings.

I'd had experience with bad improvisation, so I countered him. "No reason to be jealous," I said. "It's like the tide. It comes way in, then it goes way out."

"Well, I want to try it your way," Seth said. "I'm sick of laying these birdshit bets." He put two hundred dollars' worth of chips onto the felt.

My eyes nearly bugged out of my head. I wanted to punch him. Seth was doing everything he'd been trained not to do—and intentionally so.

Michael, his partner, looked stricken. "That's a lot of money, man," he said. "We've got to pay for our hotel tonight."

"I'm feeling lucky," said Seth. "Come on, let's do this."

I could barely pay attention to my own hand. Seth's fortunes were much more important. If he lost, then the pit bosses wouldn't care. If he won, it would be a very different story.

He got a twelve to the dealer's thirteen. Basic strategy says to hit on a twelve, but he knew the count was high. I closed my eyes and prayed for him to hit.

"Stand," he said.

Christ. The dealer flipped over her hole card. It was a jack. She'd busted.

As the two black chips came his way, a look of smugness plastered itself onto Seth's face. He pointed at me. "See, I'm as good as he is."

I wanted to bury my face in my hands. This kid's greed had exploded like an alien out of his abdomen the moment it had a chance.

But I couldn't let any of this dismay show. I was playing a character. I had to discourage him indirectly somehow.

"Man," I said, "the chances of you winning another hand like that are astronomically small."

"Not me," he said. "I'm an exception."

I forced a casual laugh. "Kid, if you keep standing on twelves, soon you'll be standing on the side of a freeway exit ramp holding a piece of cardboard."

"Whatever," he shot back.

"That's right, whatever. Do what you want."

For the next ten minutes, I watched Seth win three more hands, all on maximum bets, all on very questionable hands. He reeked of manipulation. He'd conducted ninety minutes of minimum or near-minimum bets—followed by four enormous bets, and four enormous wins. The kid had erupted into a Vesuvius of adolescent cockiness, a walking billboard for card-counting.

If I were the pit bosses, I would've busted him by now.

And then they did.

FORTY-NINE

When the goon squad appeared behind them, my palms started sweating. I tried not to look too concerned.

It consisted of two large security guards, one assistant, and one very stern pit boss.

"Young man," said the boss, "your luck has been rather fortuitous. Gather your chips, please." He nudged Michael in the back. "You too, sweetheart."

I could see the fear in the boys' eyes. "Why?" said Seth. His voice was quavering.

"You're enjoying yourself a bit too much," replied the pit boss.

"What's wrong with that?"

"We have reason to suspect that you've been counting the cards. Now gather your chips."

Michael's face had turned ashen. His hands were shaking as he scooped his chips into his pockets.

My heart went out to Michael. He hadn't asked for this. McCauley had assigned Seth to be his partner.

The pit boss waited while the boys put on their coats and put their chips into their pockets. Then he motioned with a crooked finger. A moment later, Seth and Michael were shuffling behind him, heads hung low, followed by the rest of the goon squad. I wished that I could tell the boys not to look so guilty.

They disappeared into the crowd. I turned back to the table. The dealer flipped a pair of cards at me, but I could barely look at them.

McCauley had prepared the boys for this eventuality. He'd told us that the era of being physically abused in the backrooms had ended decades ago, that those had been tactics employed by organized crime, and that only movies still used that as a plot device.

Instead, getting collared today involved three easy steps —you were first photographed, then cited for trespassing, and finally barred. The whole experience, while harmless, apparently left people intimidated. No violence necessary.

Maybe the Santa Ynez Casino was different. Maybe the Native Americans were going to beat the kids down.

I played a couple more desultory hands before collecting my winnings and slipping off my stool. My heart wasn't in it.

Instead, I wandered over to the bar and ordered a whiskey, neat, and threw it down my throat to steady my nerves. Then I began to think about the implications this had for me.

Because Seth had been collared, it meant the bosses had been watching my table. If they'd been watching my table, the bosses had surely seen my big wins, which had occurred seemingly out of the blue. That meant that I was at the top of the suspect list.

I glanced over at the pit bosses. Two of them were facing me—not directly, but almost. My stomach screwed up into a knot. The pit bosses all had earpieces. They were certainly in contact with the people manning the eye in the sky, people who were probably rewinding tape right now, noting Seth's stretches and bounces, Seth's texting, followed by my own arrival and both our big wins.

That's when I had a horrible epiphany. If I won more big bets at this casino, I'd be collared too.

I gazed across the tables. I saw Perry stretching. I saw Samuel twisting. I saw Colman bouncing seven times to the right. It was a smorgasbord of easy cash. The money may as well have been growing on trees.

Then I looked over at the pit bosses. This time, the two bosses were looking directly into my face.

I was a goose—plucked, stuffed, and trussed on a cooking sheet. All that was left to do was to give them permission to turn on the oven and slide me inside. And then I would be well and truly cooked.

That wouldn't happen. This wasn't a battle that I needed to fight. I ordered another whiskey and slammed it back fast and hard. I left a green chip for the bartender and headed down the stairs to the cashier's windows and cashed in my chips.

The team's money safely in my pockets, my head held high, I walked out the door. Echoing in my head was an old song about knowing when to hold 'em and when to fold 'em.

FIFTY

I walked back through the aisles of vines, tripping over hoses that lay like hidden snakes in the dark, waiting to attack my ankles.

A half-hour later, I arrived at the van in the tourist hamlet of Solvang. The vehicle was empty, the doors locked. Helen probably hadn't anticipated that anybody would be back so quickly. She'd most likely gone somewhere for food and drink.

I tried calling her phone, but she didn't pick up, so I wandered the streets of the touristy town. It really was a Danish wonderland. There were bakeries, cafes, knick-knack shops, antique shops, and lots of wine tasting rooms. Hordes of families swarmed the sidewalks pushing strollers and licking ice cream cones.

I found Helen inside one of the tasting rooms. There was a flight of five glasses lined up in front of her. All were filled with red wine.

"Helen," I said.

She saw me and hoisted her glass. "Oh my God, I

already joined two wine clubs tonight, and this is going to be my third. You *have* to taste this Sangiovese."

I noticed that her teeth were stained purple. She was deep into her cups. I gently pushed the glass aside. "Sorry, it looks like I'm driving home tonight."

"Oh, lighten up," she snapped. "This is the first time that I've been able to have any fun while you boys are doing your thing. Usually I'm trapped in a van listening to McCauley snore."

I watched her take another deep swig. She wiped her mouth and regarded me: "So what are you doing back so soon?"

"There was a problem."

"Ooh, how enigmatic." She mocked my voice. "*There was a problem.*"

"Seth and Michael got busted."

It took a minute, but eventually the news sunk in. Helen's eyes grew wider than dinner plates.

"Oh God, no. Where are they?"

I shrugged. She was changing before my eyes. I could see mother bear protracting her claws. She nearly reared up. "Well, we have to do *something.*"

"Like what?"

Her mouth worked itself open and shut. "I don't know. *Something.*"

"There's nothing to do except wait."

That's when my phone rang. It was Colman. "Hey, we're at the van. Where are you?"

"Give me five minutes."

The call ended. "Helen," I said, "sorry to cut your wine-tasting trip short, but they're all waiting for us."

"Let me buy just one more bottle," she said. "This one is amazing, and you can't get this in Los Angeles."

I waited for the transaction, which took forever because she couldn't decide upon which varietal. The ink wasn't even dry on the debit card receipt when I yanked her out of the store by the arm.

On the sidewalk, I took the lead. "God, you're walking so fast," she complained.

"No, you're just walking slow."

Arriving back at the van, I saw eight teenagers either leaning against it, sitting around it, or facing away from it.

"Jake," said Perry, "why the hell did you leave? I had a plus six."

"Because there was a crisis," I answered. "Did you notice a couple of us are missing?"

I took a deep breath and began to explain the state of the evening. When I'd finished, a grim silence settled upon the group.

"No way," said Perry.

"Yes way," I said, "and it happened because Seth broke the rules. He started betting the maximum, won four huge hands, and got hauled off."

"So why did you leave?" asked Colman.

"Because they were on my ass. I wasn't going to risk getting barred too."

That satisfied them. But I sensed that the team's morale was lower than a snake's belly. Samuel was crouched on a curb, head in hands.

"So what do we do now?"

Helen stumbled into the group. "There's nothing to do except wait, you dumb ass—"

I clapped my hand over her mouth and led her into the van. She laid down on one of the back benches and passed out.

I rejoined the boys and we did exactly that. We waited.

In fact, it was another hour before Seth and Michael finally materialized out of the dark vineyards. They looked disheveled, frightened, but unharmed.

The other boys surrounded the pair as though they'd just wandered in after a successful desert crossing. I watched the commotion, the backslaps, the high fives, the fist bumps.

Then I stepped in. "Seth."

"Jake," he replied coolly.

"Why did you start betting big?"

"I didn't," he said.

"Don't lie," I said. "You know good and hell well what happened in there was your fault. Now keep your mouth shut while I talk to your partner."

I turned towards Michael. "Tell us about the backstage shenanigans."

I could see that Michael was more shaken up. After all, he wasn't anywhere near the sociopath that Seth was.

"God," he said, "it was scary. First they sat us down at separate tables in separate rooms. They harassed the shit out of us. They took our IDs and asked me to repeat all the information on it. They said they knew we were working as a team. They wanted to know who was the leader."

Then he looked directly at me. "And they wanted to know who you were, Jake."

"Tell me that you didn't tell them."

"Hell no," he replied. "I said I'd never seen you in my life."

"Anything else?" I said.

"They took my phone and looked through the text messages. They took pictures of ones that they wanted. But don't worry."

I turned back to Seth. "Did they do the same to you?"

The skeezy kid nodded.

"Did they take your phone?"

He nodded again. I felt my stomach begin to drop. "And did they look through your text messages?"

"Yeah," he said. "They took some pictures."

"Let me see your phone."

He handed it over. I thumbed through the sent messages folder. Then I stopped. There it was.

"Maybe this one?"

I lifted up his phone and showed him his own sent message.

To: Jake Logan
Sent: January 13, 6:41 pm
Message: +4

"Yes," Seth said.

My stomach hit the floor. These kids all had fake names on their fake identification. But this was a different story.

The anger exploded out of my mouth. "You *idiot*," I said. "You had my *real* name in your phone. And you texted me the count—not even in code, either, but the actual number. And now the pit bosses probably saw it."

Seth shrugged. He was unmoved. I saw everything unspooling in my head. My name and face, Jake Logan, wasn't exactly private, not after almost a decade of acting gigs in Hollywood. A simple search engine inquiry would match my name to my face in a fraction of a second. Then casino security could match up their internal video footage to my various acting roles, all of which were freely available.

I was toast. The next time I tried to enter a casino, the security would be watching me so hard that my hands would burst into flames.

FIFTY-ONE

"Seth," I said, "do you have *any* idea how *badly* you just screwed yourself?"

"It's all good," he replied.

"No, it's *not* good. You know the worst part?"

"What?"

"You just screwed your teammates."

"No, I didn't," he said.

I was annoyed by his adolescent logic. It was mostly denial and rationalization.

Michael couldn't bite his tongue anymore. "Stop lying, man. I saw them photograph you. And you got the same trespassing citation I did."

"No, I didn't," said Seth.

The group's attention was fixed on Seth, but he wasn't going to crack. His mental health depended upon it.

I'd finally had enough. I decided to exercise my unspoken authority. "Seth, you're off the team," I said. "Not that it matters. You're about to be barred from every casino in the state anyways."

He looked shocked. "You can't kick me off the team."

"McCauley would've done the same," I said. "You've put all of us at risk. Simple as that."

"Screw off, Jake," he said.

"No, *you* can screw off. You broke the goddamn rules."

"No, I didn't."

I slapped my forehead. "Seth, I was *right there*." I turned to Michael. "So were you! What did Seth do?"

"He broke the rules," Michael said.

Seth's nostrils flared. He stepped backwards from the group. "I'm the best counter on this team. If I go, then you guys will collapse."

"Whatever," said Colman. "We can win money without you, Seth."

"There's not even going to *be* any money," Seth fired back. "McCauley's laying drunk somewhere. Without him, this team won't survive, and there won't be any more investment in the trust. We're the last class. We won't get the payout."

Seth might be right about all that. I'd had the same fears. But I didn't agree with his attempts at a scorched-earth, slippery-slope method of persuasion.

"Plus," he continued, "if you kick me off the team, I'm going to tell the authorities."

That was a dumb thing to say. He was surrounded by nine other boys whose future financial solvency depended upon the team. I was happy to see them react appropriately. I listened to the cries, watched the hands reach out and shove the offender backwards.

Seth stumbled backwards, away from the group. He punched the air, a hundred and fifty pounds of hostility and ego.

"I'm serious," he said. "I'll blow the whistle on this whole program. My family doesn't even need the money anyways."

Keep telling yourself that, I thought.

"In fact," he said, "I'll make my own team."

"Forget it," said Michael. "You're *barred*."

"So I'll wear a disguise. We don't need McCauley or Helen or this joker"—he pointed at me—"all taking a cut of the pie. We can get more on our own. So who's coming with me?"

He raised his hand and looked around the group. I tried not to laugh. It was a ludicrous teenage dream, a me-against-the-world kind of scheme that would collapse under the weight of a fake mustache. I decided to let it ride.

We glanced around. Nobody raised a hand.

"You're all insane," said Michael. "A bunch of pussies. Me, I was just trying to earn us some extra money. I was doing it for the *group*. You don't want my help, fine. I'll do it on my own. Have a good life."

Seth turned away and walked into the darkness. We all watched him go. The guys were shell-shocked. Nobody spoke.

Finally Perry broke the silence. "Should we wait for him after he's cooled off?"

"It doesn't matter," I said. "He's off the team. Let's go."

"We can't just leave him here?"

"It's his choice," I said. "He'll get home somehow. But it's not our business anymore."

I slid behind the wheel and started the engine. "Come on, guys."

The boys sadly climbed into the van, arranging themselves around Helen's unconscious body, and shut the door.

Michael took the passenger seat. I threw the shifter into drive and carried the team out of Solvang, back to Los Angeles.

FIFTY-TWO

"That's not exactly what happened, ma'am," I heard myself saying into the phone. "Yes, I will explain what exactly happened, if you would be quiet for a moment."

I was pacing circles on the floor of my living room with my phone to my ear. It had been ringing all morning. The angry parents of team members had wanted to know all about what happened to McCauley, what happened in Santa Ynez, what was happening to the team.

I had few answers. But I'd found myself the point man, since the parents wouldn't dare call the high school, and because Helen had wisely left her number unlisted. It felt like working at an automobile company whose engines kept exploding.

Now I was having the types of intimate conversations that you heard at parent-teacher conferences. Colman's mother explained to me why she would hold me personally responsible for the impending family bankruptcy. Samuel's father offered to break my limbs if I didn't master basic strategy. Perry's older sister painted a bleak Dickensian portrait of future family Christmases, complete with a handicapped youngest child, if this team didn't come through.

By two o'clock, my phone's battery had died. I had just plugged it into its charger when it began ringing again.

I frowned and looked at the caller. It was from Xavier High School.

I picked up quickly. "McCauley?"

"Don't you wish," said the reedy, scholastic voice. It was Father James.

"Yes, Father," I replied.

"The grapevine says you had a bit of a problem amongst the grapevines. Pardon the pun."

"That wasn't a pun," I said. "And as long as you're asking, yes, Seth got himself and Michael barred from the casino. Then he refused to admit that he'd done anything wrong. Then he threatened to sink the entire team. So I kicked him off."

"That's not what his mother's saying. She's saying you left him in Santa Ynez."

"I did. He threatened to destroy the team."

"His mom had to drive to Santa Ynez to pick him up."

"That's too bad."

"She thinks you should've driven her son home."

"I think that apple hasn't fallen too far from the tree."

The priest sounded upset. "Jake, you've got to figure this out. I'll take care of mom best I can, but the last thing Xavier High School needs is for this to become public."

I sighed. "I'm trying to hold this team together, but McCauley blackmailed me into joining to begin with. The boys don't have much respect for me."

He made a small grunt of acknowledgement. "So what do you think would solve all these problems?"

"Having McCauley back."

There was a silence on the other end of the phone. I can tell the type of silence—a scared silence, an angry silence, a bored silence. This was a silence that was pregnant with unspoken information.

"You won't get him back."

It felt like there was more dirt, so I stuck my shovel into it and dug hard. "It sounds like you know where he is."

"He's been located, yes."

My heart skipped a beat. "When?"

"Two days ago."

"Where?"

"That's immaterial. He's safe now."

"Tell me where."

The priest's voice sounded strained. "Not possible, Jake."

"But I'd like to talk to him."

"He might not be lucid."

"I'll wait."

"That could be a while."

"I'm used to it. I'm an actor. I've waited months for a callback."

He blew air out of his mouth. "If I tell you, I could get in trouble."

"You didn't tell me anything. You don't even know me. Nobody knows anything. Haven't you seen any mob movies?"

"You won't breathe a word?" he said.

"*Silencio*," I said.

"McCauley is at Manresa, undergoing rehabilitation," he said. Then added: "A spiritual one."

My ear perked up. Father James had mentioned Manresa in his office a few days earlier. It was the Jesuit retirement home.

"I'll pay him a visit," I said.

"It won't be pretty. He's in bad shape."

I smirked. "I'll put a paper bag over his head."

"If you used plastic, you would probably be doing him a favor."

I stifled a laugh. There were some thoughts you shouldn't ever hear a holy man say out loud.

"Here's one way to shut up Seth's mom," I said. "Tell her to try to take her son into a casino tonight."

"She probably would. She worships the little bastard. Take care."

I ended the call and looked at my phone's display. There'd been three missed calls from three different parents during our brief conversation.

I put the phone on silent, then began to get dressed. I needed to find Manresa.

FIFTY-THREE

I spread out the Thomas Guide on the passenger seat of my car, put my thermos of hot tea on top of the loose change in my cup holder, and began to drive eastwards across Los Angeles.

It was a dark, stormy winter's day, typical of January in Southern California. Outsiders have the irrational vision of Los Angeles as a temperate paradise, but what they don't realize is that it gets downright cold here. For some surfers, it's year-round wetsuit weather, even in the summer.

A quick Internet search had yielded the news— Manresa, the regional Jesuit retirement home, could be found in an old mansion located in the foothills of Altadena. My foot on the accelerator, I leaned forward and peered out through my windshield to the sky. It was a gunmetal gray, clouds angrily billowing like the wrath of God. I turned on my headlights. It was barely eleven am.

Forty miles later and twice as many minutes later, I turned off the freeway. The road passed through a quaint downtown. I hadn't known this was here. It was easy to not know anything was anywhere in Los Angeles. It's a city of nooks and crannies.

The road weaved its way alongside a creek, then banked up the side of the first foothill. The pine grove smelled fresh and crisp. Then I remembered that most such pines were zombie trees, killed by the bark beetle epidemic, yet still standing. It was a forest of tinder.

The trees would fall someday. It was only a matter of time.

The road kept climbing, and ten minutes later it swept around a hairpin turn that offered a dizzying view of the floor of the valley to the left. I tried to keep my tires on the asphalt.

At last a sign came into view. It was made of rocks and timber. In rough-hewn letters I could see the word *Manresa*.

I pulled up to the gate. There was an intercom with a button. I pushed it, and the gate swung open. Just like that. They didn't need much security here. The Jesuits had probably figured that ninety-year-old priests in wheelchairs had nothing to offer venal and worldly outsiders.

I accelerated slowly up the winding driveway, through another stand of pines, until the building came into view.

It was an old hillside lodge that had been purchased and refurbished by the Jesuits half a century ago. I stepped out of my car and studied the edifice. It looked like little had been done since then. The chinking mortar between the dark logs was crumbling. The roof was as patchy as a teenager's beard. And the gauzy curtains in the windows looked yellowed enough to have been original.

I trudged up the steps and found myself on a rustic porch. Nearby, in a rocking chair, was an old man swaddled in Pendleton blankets. His stubbly-white chin was tucked tightly into his chest and his eyes were closed.

I tiptoed past him and pulled open the front screen door. When the hinge squeaked, the old man jerked awake.

"Lunch time?" he said.

I froze. "It sure is. What do you want me to bring you?"

"Chocolate pudding. Not the hazelnut."

"Comin' right up."

No sooner had the words left his mouth than his chin had plunged once more into his chest and his eyelids had crashed.

The main entry to Manresa hadn't changed from its days as a hillside hotel. The large lobby was strewn with heavy couches and chairs. Ten old men in sweaters and gloves lay dozing next to a roaring fire in a hearth. That made sense. This lodge probably hadn't been built to modern heating specs.

The medical station was next to the door. I guessed that it used to be the front desk. A large maroon-and-gold shield hung on the wall. I peered closely. A pair of wolves seemed to be hanging onto a pot in the upper right and lower left quadrants.

"That's the Loyola family crest," said a voice.

I turned. Behind me was a very young Jesuit, twenty-three if he was a day, dressed in black pants and a red sweater. This difference, however, was that this one stood about six and a half feet high. I could see his forearms bulging beneath the sweater.

"It's interesting," I replied. "Who made it?"

He narrowed his eyes. "I'm not a docent."

"With an attitude like that, you'll stay that way."

He sighed. "I'm bored, so I'll ask. What do you want?"

I thought about that. I'd skipped lunch, and what I really wanted was a hamburger with sautéed mushrooms and melted smoked gouda. Instead, I told him something else.

"Patrick McCauley."

He lifted an eyebrow. "Father McCauley is unavailable."

This is where I would normally have slapped some sort of bill on the table and said something snarky. However, this man was a priest. He was a man of God. He'd supposedly conquered all known appetites.

I played at looking sad. "When will he be available?"

"Whenever he stops shaking and puking."

So it was that bad. He'd been here for two days, but detoxing from booze could take four days. I didn't like the idea of spending two leisurely days here.

I spun around and tried to look helpless. This Jesuit, after all, could pound me down into the fires of hell.

"Well," I said, "what do you guys do around here for fun?"

The answer came swiftly: "We pray. We drink. We play board games."

One of those didn't fit with the others. I decided to play it coy. "You got chess?"

"Yep."

"You any good?"

"Nobody here's beat me so far."

"Your competition isn't exactly on their feet." I nodded at the sound of snoring in the room behind him. "And we've both got a rainy day. I say we play best two out of three. Or until McCauley wakes up. Don't worry, I'm no good."

Those were the magic words. He instantly let down his guard. "Yeah, man, why not. You like whiskey?"

FIFTY-FOUR

The empty shot glass landed on the small table with a thud. My opponent and I were facing each other over a chess board.

I'd found out that he was a seminarian, not yet a full priest, and that he was twenty-four years old. He was midway through a yearlong assignment here. I wondered who didn't like him.

"Do you really want to do that?" my opponent said. He was pointing at my bishop. It was at the edge of the board.

"Why not?"

"Bishops on the rim are grim."

"Oh."

I moved it to a different place. I was playing good at playing dumb. I asked stupid questions, spaced out, tried to move his pieces, got distracted by bright shiny things.

"This is a massacre," said the seminarian. "I'm buying you a strategy book for Christmas."

"Maybe I'm just not Russian enough."

"Or autistic."

I liked the cut of his jib and poured him another shot of

whiskey. "You're pretty real for a priest. You like to get your hands dirty."

"That's the thing about Jesuits," he replied. "We're practical bastards. You ever hear that joke?"

I shook my head and poured myself another shot. I needed it for what I was about to do to him. "No, tell me."

He cleared his throat. "So a Franciscan, a Dominican, and a Jesuit are celebrating Mass together when the lights suddenly go out. So what do they all do? The Franciscan thanks God for the chance to live more simply. The Dominican gives a homily on how God brings light to the world."

"And the Jesuit?" I said.

"He goes downstairs into the basement and fixes the fuse box."

It was a good joke. So was this game. In less than fifteen minutes, I'd found myself on the frantic end of cat-and-mouse. I had nothing left except a pawn and a king.

"Check," said the seminarian, "for the eighth time. You really want to prolong this?"

"Not really," I said. "Tell you what, let's play one more. I promise to pay better attention. If I win, you have to let me see McCauley."

"Sounds good."

"Swear to God."

He lifted his meaty hand. "I swear on all that is holy to defeat you."

I poured him another shot. It was his fifth one, and he wasn't saying no. There wasn't much else to do out here in this nowhere retirement home with a bunch of ancient doddering priests slumbering in easy chairs all around.

As he set up the pieces, I admired the boardwork. "I feel like I'm learning so much about this game from you."

"It'd be hard not to," he answered.

The seminarian led with a strong queen. That was a street move. I wondered if he'd learned to play in a public park.

I led with a purposefully weak move, exposing my king. The seminarian shook his head. "I could spin this board around and play with your pieces and still beat you. That's how bad you are."

Suddenly I could see him without the collar. Deep within his breast lay the beating heart of a boastful, swaggering young man. "Aww, be nice," I said. "Here, what if I do this."

I slid my rook across the board into perfect position. He cocked his head. I could see him taking in all the implications. "That was ... unexpected."

"Was it?" I said.

"I can't tell if it was by accident or design."

He paused a moment—and then moved his knight exactly where I'd expected him to. I'd already planned my next move, but I hemmed and hawed for a minute more, to make it look like an accident. My hand finally slid my bishop around the back of his defensive structure.

"What the hell," he said.

"Was that a good move too?" I said, blinking innocently.

"It could be, if you knew where it could lead."

He played the expected defensive move. I was ready for that too and countered it. "How's that?"

Now the seminarian was sweating. See, the key to hustling somebody is that you don't change behavior. You keep up the innocent act from soup to nuts. That's how you keep yourself from being beaten half to death in a back alley later.

"I don't know ..." His speech was slurring. The whiskey was helping my cause.

Twenty minutes later, I had backed him into the final corner. "Check," I said, "and mate." Then I leaned back, holding my head in my hands, mimicking shock. "How did that happen?"

"I have no clue."

"Maybe you drank too much."

His eyes fixed upon mine. "Maybe you should get upstairs to room two-oh-three before I forget about my vows."

I smiled. "Which one—poverty, chastity, or obedience? Because if you're somehow getting rich or getting laid, maybe we can still be friends."

"The fourth one. The vow of nonviolence." He cracked his knuckles.

That settled it. This seminarian had been raised on the streets. And he had seen through my little charade. I thought about rubbing in the truth—that I'd been a citywide chess champion at age nine—then thought better of it.

He swiped the pieces off the board and reached for the whiskey bottle. I stood up and quickly moved towards the staircase.

FIFTY-FIVE

"Jake who?" said the voice behind the door marked 203.

I was standing in the long, carpeted, second-floor hall-way. At the end, a frosted glass window let in what little natural light there was. It had taken a minute and a half of knocking on his door and pleading to get McCauley to say these two words.

"Jake Logan," I said. "The sweeper. On the team."

A pause. Then: "Oh."

"Can you open the door?"

"Not for you."

I frowned. I was fed up. I hadn't driven fifty miles in the pouring rain and hustled a seminarian at chess for nothing. I put my hand on the doorknob and turned it and pushed inside.

The bedroom was smaller than a mouse dropping. It had one chair, one desk, one desk lamp, and one single bed. Nothing else. The floor was linoleum. An old radiator hissed in the corner.

McCauley was in the bed, under the sheets, as still as a corpse. He was wearing an old-school wifebeater tank top undershirt. A garbage can sat on the floor next to him. The room smelled of stale vomit and disinfectant.

I flipped on the desk lamp to get a better look at him. I was sorry that I had. The old priest seemed to have aged a decade in the past week.

His fingers clutched the edge of the sheets on his chest. "Jesus Christ," he said. "You shouldn't have come here."

I pulled up the chair. "You shouldn't have walked out on us."

"I didn't have a choice."

That was odd. I peered at him. His mouth was working itself open and shut, like a dying fish.

"This is a really small room," I said.

He nodded. "I have to go out into the hall just to change my mind."

Even in the throes of withdrawal, he still had that snappy Irish wit. I decided to drop the pretense. "So tell me about the bender. Was it worth it?"

McCauley struggled up to a sitting position in bed. "Well, it didn't end in handcuffs, so it wasn't my best performance."

He grinned at me, but I wasn't laughing. I'd watched alcoholism destroy the careers of a lot of older actors. Nobody coddled substance abusers as well as the entertainment industry.

"You can't live like this," I said.

"I can't live any other way," he replied. Then he grew angry. "I've got plenty of men telling me how to live my life, Jake. I hope you're here to tell me something different."

"The team is falling apart. We need you to come back."

He looked profoundly distressed. "I can't."

"Seth got barred at Santa Ynez this weekend. He broke all the rules and I kicked him off the team."

The priest shrugged. "There's always one like that. He had it coming anyways. I predicted that back in September."

"Michael got barred with him."

The old priest looked pained but didn't say anything.

"You have to finish the rest of the year," I said.

He shook his head. "I can't. Literally—I'm not allowed out for the next month. In fact, I'm scheduled to begin the Spiritual Exercises next Monday. It's four weeks of deep contemplation. After that, they're going to reassign me."

"To where?"

He took an index finger and pointed it straight down to the floor. "Probably here. It's the end of the line." He sighed. "Too many missed classes. Too many obvious hangovers. Too many birthdays."

Father James had warned me that this might happen. We spent a minute listening to the small clicks of the radiator.

I finally cleared my throat. "So the team is finished."

"Unless *you* want to run it."

The old priest's eyes were searching my face. Stammering, I rejected the offer. "It's impossible. I don't know how I would build a stake each year. Your friends are priests who donate their monthly stipends. My friends are a bunch of self-absorbed actors with ten cents to their names."

"Yeah," he said, "I figured as much."

"Besides, I don't know how to count cards, and the parents wouldn't trust me. Not the way they trust you."

"It's the collar," he said. "It works magic."

I grew more impassioned. "Father McCauley, without you, the team can't exist. You're the glue."

That was the truth. He looked pensive. Then he settled

back into his pillow and shifted his gaze over to the wall behind my head.

I thought of Michael, and his mother, and their disappointment. They were depending upon this money for college.

He seemed to read my mind. "I talked to Helen this morning. She tells me that we have enough in the trust to pay out all current college students—but not enough for this class."

"We're still at half a million, right?"

He nodded. "And we still need two hundred thousand dollars more. But"—he held up a finger—"Helen has found a new index fund somewhere in Europe that's paying outrageously well. Don't ask the name. It's all very hush-hush."

"So?"

"She thinks that with increased exposure to that fund, we could lower this year's goal to six hundred thousand. In which case, we're only one hundred thousand short."

That was still a lot of gambling. On our best night, we'd only pulled in about fifteen thousand dollars. And we were going to be playing one table down from now on.

"I'm willing to keep trying," I said.

"Of course you are."

"Not just for the commission."

"Oh, right. You don't want to be dinged as a kiddie-diddler."

That reptilian smirk appeared on his face. I lost my patience. "Oh, for Christ's sake, McCauley—do I have to spell it out? I *care* about these kids."

He looked amused. "Ah ha. It took four months for the real Jake to finally reveal himself."

"What's that supposed to mean?"

"Under the self-absorbed actor bullshit, he's actually an idealist."

I bristled at the mockery. "You're an idealist too, McCauley. Otherwise you wouldn't have been using all these dirty tricks to help poor kids."

The old priest didn't say anything to that. Instead, he reached for his glass of water with shaking hand. His lips sucked greedily from the rim.

He set down the glass. "So Helen's been monitoring the casinos in my absence," he said. "She tells me that Temecula just instituted one- and two-deck games. With deep penetration. The same two-hundred-dollar maximum."

I shrugged. "You said we don't do those games. You said that they're honeypots for shitty counters."

"But you could try," he said, a conspiratorial glint in his eye, "if you want to make that money in one night."

I laughed. "A hundred thousand in one night? On twenty-dollar minimum tables? With no special deals? It's impossible. I'd be barred for sure."

He leaned forward and lowered his voice. "Even if you do get caught, it's nothing to be afraid of."

"But I wouldn't be able to help the team after that."

He squeezed the bridge of his nose between his fingers, squinching his eyes shut. "The team is finished, Jake. I'm going to be here for the rest of my life, trying to discern my disordered affections."

I didn't understand that lingo, so I kept him on track. "Do you think we ought to try that game in Temecula?"

The priest nodded. "Go big. The count is going to get real high, real fast. If we're going to hit one hundred thousand in a night, we'll need multiple hands being bet at maximum. Tell the kids to forget about steaming. Everybody bets according to the count. And, most importantly, we need to assign one kid to run around and discreetly collect the chips and take them off premises. Just in case."

Something in his language pricked up my ears. The first-person plural.

"I'm ready to go right now," I said. "C'mon, I'll give you a lift."

"I'm not going anywhere."

"But you said *we*." I picked up his shoes from the floor. "And there's still some miles left on these tires."

He shook his head. "If you're lucky, Jake, you'll learn what it's like to be seventy-seven years old. I can't go."

It was no use. McCauley was a mountain; I was a kid throwing pebbles at it. I stood up and stretched. Going to Temecula sounded like a crazy plan, one that would likely see all of us barred— but if it would get a college education for Michael, I was willing to try.

"You could do it on Wednesday," he suggested. "That way you avoid the scummy strokers who drive in for the weekend from out-of-town."

"Sounds good."

"Let me know what happens." Something in his voice sounded wistful.

"I will. Goodbye, Father McCauley."

He didn't say anything. But as the door clicked shut behind me, in the silence that weighed more than a thousand words, I thought I heard a tiny, choked goodbye.

FIFTY-SIX

"I have three major announcements," I said.

The team was ripping through rural California on the way to Temecula. It was five o'clock pm on a Wednesday. My hands gripped the wheel. My stomach had tied itself into a twisted bag of acid.

Behind me, nine pairs of ears awaited the news. Next to me, Helen was applying lipstick in the mirror on the visor. Everyone knew about my conversation with McCauley. Everyone knew that this was the team's grand finale.

"Number one," I said. "Since we're aiming for a hundred grand, Helen will be sweeping with me tonight. It'll double our renewal."

The boys clapped. They'd been asking her all year to hit the floor of the casino. "The cougar is on the prowl," said Perry.

"Ew," said Colman.

Helen whirled around. "I'll have you know that I'm wanted from coast to coast like butter and toast." Then she turned back in her seat.

I raised my voice. "Number two, we're finished

steaming."

The statement was greeted with silence. The boys were a hard, dry desert pan. I was a wanderer with a watering can. This one would take a while to sink in.

Then Perry understood. "You want us to stop steaming?"

"Yes," I said.

"We can bet whatever we want?"

"Yes."

"Won't we get caught?"

"Probably. But if McCauley isn't coming back, we're disbanding. And we're never going to see a game like this again."

"One- or two-deck games," added Helen. "Full penetration."

Normally, a van full of teenage boys would be making jokes about those last two words. But they knew this was serious. They'd witnessed firsthand how much money could be generated at blackjack. They were depending upon this to avoid future loans.

"Wow," said Samuel.

"See, boys, the goalposts have been pushed forward," said Helen. "We only need a hundred grand more, and your educations will be covered."

"Why is that?"

I waited for that response. I figured it might involve words such as *insider* and *trading*. "Oh," she said breezily, "don't ask too many questions. And with Seth gone, our responsibility is lowered further."

The van grew even more silent. That statement sunk in quicker than the last one had. My booting Seth off the team had a pleasant effect—it meant that we would have to win much less money.

"Speaking of which, did anybody talk to him this week?" I asked.

"I did," said Michael.

"What did he say?"

"He said he hated us and especially you. He hates Father McCauley too."

That was expected. "Did you tell him that we were coming to Temecula?" Michael didn't respond. I looked at him in the rearview. "Did you?"

"No," replied Michael.

I didn't believe him. I thought hard as we cruised through the rolling hills towards Temecula.

"Third and last announcement," I said. "Michael is going to be joining us on the floor of the casino."

"I am?" said Michael. "But I've been banned."

He was genuinely surprised. He'd been photographed and banned already. He basically was along for the ride tonight.

"Not if you wear this." Helen tossed him a cowboy hat. "And your sunglasses."

"In the casino?" he said.

"You've got a vision problem," I said. "You also didn't deserve to get collared last week. So tonight you're going to be playing a new position. Let's call it *rover*."

"Woof woof," said Samuel.

Michael was excited. "What do I do?"

"Play fetch. With money."

Helen stepped in. "Tonight you'll be the annoying friend who wanders around stupidly, pestering your friends at other tables. Boys, shove your chips at him and tell him to go buy something. Michael, you come back to the van and drop them off. Then repeat."

Michael nodded. I could tell that he thought this would

be fun.

"The rest of you," I said, "keep as few chips on the table or on your person as possible."

The implication was clear. The atmosphere in the van quickly grew tense.

An hour later, we arrived in Temecula, and I parked in the same place as we had weeks earlier. "Once we start, nothing stops us except exhaustion or security. All other rules still apply. Got it?"

The boys nodded.

"Eat quickly at the buffet before you start. You'll need the energy. Don't get so excited that you forget to throw me and Helen signals. Remember that she and I aren't counting."

I watched the boys pile out of the van and head down the sidewalk. Michael hung around me and Helen. Then I realized why. I handed him the key to the van. "Here you go. You'll look good in a cowboy hat."

He glanced down the street. The casino was half a mile away. "Now I know why you told me to wear my sneakers. I'm going to lose five pounds tonight." He exhaled and looked around. "This feels different without a partner. Scarier."

"You told Seth that we were coming here tonight, didn't you?"

Michael hung his head guiltily. I'd seen through his lie. But what I didn't know was whether or not it could hurt us. Seth would be capable of anything.

"Go eat," I said. "Then get ready to run."

Michael turned and trundled along the sidewalk. I saw Helen had her phone to her ear. "Who are you calling?"

"McCauley," she replied. "He needs to know about Seth."

FIFTY-SEVEN

Nearly four hours later, eight columns of black and red chips stood on the green table like a miniature Parthenon.

The Temecula Casino had, nearly overnight, become shockingly friendly to counters. I didn't know why they'd changed the rules. Helen had said that it was a seasonal promotion.

All I knew was that I was playing a two-deck game, and that the penetration was exceptional. The dealer was diving nearly the bottom of the shoe. Normally you'd have to tip the dealers a lot to do the same, but this time it was *gratis*. Whatever their motivation, there was no denying that it was the best game I'd ever seen.

Still, I hadn't been able to forget tangling with this casino staff weeks ago. I'd been here with the skanks, Thelma and Velma, and been chased through the adjacent hotel. The picture of the girl laying naked on the sheets hadn't exactly been easy to erase from my mind either. I'd been happy when McCauley had agreed to drop them from the team.

Now McCauley had dropped himself.

I looked at my chips. They amounted to at least eight thousand dollars. Michael was taking his sweet time to get over to me. I'd seen him cruising around with a new Jansport backpack, pretending to annoy his winning friends while discreetly hauling their pieces away from the floor, out the door, and into the van. If the other tables were doing this well, we'd probably won forty thousand dollars in chips by now.

I sat out the next hand and leaned back and stretched. It's good to take a break sometimes. My eyes roved the room and landed on Helen. I could see her resisting the attentions of an older man. He had his arms wrapped around her. On the green felt was a stack of chips as high as my own. Part of me wondered why we hadn't used her earlier.

Then I saw the wolf-man.

He was standing in a suit next to the pit bosses. He hadn't been there a few minutes earlier. And he looked more predatory, if that were even possible, than last time—his eyes beadier, his snout longer, his teeth sharper.

Then the wolf-man swung his head around, and his red little eyes landed upon me. I could feel my internal organs shrinking back into my trunk. But I was wearing a small disguise. I'd bought a straw cowboy hat and pair of sunglasses in the gift shop just before hitting the tables.

Until now, I hadn't needed any wigs or such ludicrousness, but that's because the team hadn't needed to hit the same the casino twice to win big money. So far, my only second visits had been to purposefully lose. Here, though, my purpose was to win, and so I needed to be more careful. The bosses were watching these games like hawks anyways.

The wolf-man looked at my table, looked at my pile of chips, then studied my face. I yawned lazily and pretended to inspect a fingernail. I shared small talk with the woman to my left.

The wolf-man moved on.

My thespian skills had worked. Or maybe it was that I didn't look that unusual. Once glance around the tables told me that there were at least twenty other guys playing with caps and sunglasses on. I guessed that they were all counters.

Then the dealer said, "That's it for this shoe."

I creased my brow. This was a double-deck game, and he'd only penetrated halfway.

"Come on," I said, "this table's hot," I said. "Keep it going."

"No can do," he said.

"Sure you can." I tossed him a green chip.

He caught the chip and slipped it into his pocket. Then he dumped the shoe out anyways. "Thanks."

I frowned but understood. He'd been delivered new orders. The bosses were controlling our winnings by changing the penetration, like engineers controlling the hydraulic flow of water out of a dam. They knew good and hell well that they were attracting counters with this type of game, but they weren't letting most of us take it all home. I didn't know why. Maybe the casino wanted to get a facial profile on all possible counters in the state of California.

This was a honeypot indeed.

I looked at my Parthenon again. They'd let me play long. The same went for Helen. There must be a reason.

"Then I'm done here," I told him. "There's no way the next shoe can be that hot."

I started to sweep all my chips into my pockets. I felt the dealer watching me. "You want a bag?" he said. "That's a lot of chips."

That was a nice offer, one of the small perks offered to winners. "Sure," I said.

He handed me a simple plastic sack with a cinch top. The words *Temecula Casino* were marked on the side. I dumped my chips into the sack and closed it tightly, then held it by the mouth as I left the table.

I swaggered through the tables, toothpick in my teeth, bag hooked onto my belt. If they hadn't busted me yet, they probably wouldn't do so. I was free to relocate to another table. I saw Colman signal a plus four. There was a free seat at either end of his table. I chose the one on the right and slung my bag of chips onto the green felt.

"Howdy," I said.

The dealer nodded at me. As he started to deal, I saw someone slide onto the open seat on the left. I turned my head—and immediately felt like I'd just been punched in the gut.

It was Seth.

FIFTY-EIGHT

I felt invisible hands reach down my throat and yank the breath out of my lungs. It wasn't a sensation that I would recommend.

Seth was staring right at me. He wore a brand-new black suit with a red silk shirt and a red pocket square. He looked like the devil in adolescent form.

"Let's get this show on the road," he said to the dealer. "I'm ready to see some winning." He spotted my bag. "It looks like you've been pretty successful already."

My nostrils flared without permission. My molars began to grind one another into powder. I struggled to keep a straight face. There could only be two reasons for his presence: greed or revenge.

"Yeah, there was a hot table over there, and I just kept riding it," I said.

He scratched his head. "Haven't I seen you before?"

"Nope."

"I think I have. You weren't wearing the hat or sunglasses."

So there was the motive: revenge. I felt my inner

Grendel gnash its teeth. I envisioned leaping across the table and tearing his torso in half and feasting on the innards.

"Tell you what," I said. "You work your side of the table, and I'll work mine."

He didn't say anything to that. We played the first hand. Colman and I both won. Seth busted.

"This guy and his luck," he said, jerking a thumb at me. "It just never ends."

"Kind of like your mouth," I shot back.

"Or your mother's."

The second hand came out. I stood on a twelve and won two hundred dollars. Seth busted again. His eyes were pure malevolence.

"If you keep standing on twelves," he said, "soon you'll be standing on the side of a freeway exit ramp holding a piece of cardboard."

Those words sounded familiar. That was because they had been my own. I shook them off with a wave of my hand. "Actually, I've just gotten—"

"—really lucky," he said, interrupting. "How does that happen, exactly? Enough to make ten thousand dollars? At this casino? At Santa Ynez? At Ventura?"

I noticed the dealer eavesdropping on our conversation with interest. His job wasn't to catch card counters, not explicitly, but the bosses probably made it in his best interest.

Colman had noticed the dealer's attention too. He quietly gathered his chips into his pockets and left. I watched him stroll to the far end of the gambling floor and take up residence at a different table.

As the dealer flipped out his cards, I chewed over my options. There weren't many. Ignoring Seth was no longer an option. I could play dumb. I could pay him off. I could trade snappy insults. I could coldcock him. Or I could leave.

None of them were viable. My gut told me to leave, but Seth was just going to follow me to other tables. His whole purpose here was to sabotage the team, and specifically me, until we all got collared and banned. And that could decide whether Michael, who was a second-string player in the last year of the team's history, would get financial assistance for college or not.

I couldn't let that happen.

While I was trying to figure out my next move, I felt a heavy presence approach behind me, something old and large. As its shadow passed across my back, the hair on my neck pricked up. The gambling floor suddenly seemed to grow colder.

"Anybody got room here for an old man?" said a deep voice.

A chill ran down my spine. I knew that voice. And as I twisted around, I realized that I'd been expecting to hear it all along.

It was Father McCauley.

FIFTY-NINE

The card-counting priest slid onto the middle of the five seats. He wasn't wearing a disguise. He wasn't wearing a Roman collar either. McCauley just looked like any other old man sidling up to a table.

Which was exactly his intention.

I glanced over to suss out the old man's health. His cheeks seemed ruddy. His hair was mussed up. His eyes were a little unfocused. In his hand was a glass of brown liquid. It looked like whiskey.

I shook my head. There went the rehab, the empty room with the clicking radiator, the four weeks of spiritual discernment.

I twiddled a chip between my thumbs. I'd spent months ignoring my own teammates at blackjack tables, but this was going to be much different. It would be hard to ignore McCauley. He was a superstar to those of us in the know.

I glanced down. On the floor, near McCauley's feet, was a black Jansport backpack. It was new, and I could tell it was empty from the way it was crumpled. That was the exact same bag that Michael had just bought. I smiled to myself. He'd already scouted us. He'd noted Michael's purchase, then bought an identical copy. And he was waiting for me to notice.

The Jesuit's forethought was diabolical.

Across the table, Seth's eyes had bugged out of his skull. It was no surprise. If I were in his place, I'd be shitting myself too.

I watched McCauley reach into his pocket and feebly withdrew two black chips. He placed them carefully on the square of green felt. I'd never seen him move so slowly. It wasn't clear if it was an act, either.

"Is that going to be enough?" he said innocently.

"Oh yes," said the dealer. "That's the maximum, actually."

"Should I leave it?" said McCauley. "I can take one back. What should I do?" He looked to the dealer for advice.

"Your choice," said the dealer.

"You should take it back," said Seth.

"No, I think he should leave it," I said. "It could be his lucky day."

The kid and I stared daggers at one another. Meanwhile, the dealer had ignored us and started the hand, so McCauley's two hundred dollars stayed.

As the play began, I tried to ignore McCauley's little antics, but it was tough. He played the doddering old man perfectly. He looked around at other people's hands. He fussed over his cards, pretending to be indecisive. He wiped his forehead with his wrist. If the man ever got booted from the priesthood, which wasn't impossible, he could have a second career as an actor.

"Hey, look at that," McCauley said. "I won."

The dealer smirked as he shoved a couple more black

chips at the old man. McCauley wore a huge dumb grin as he looked around the table for approval.

"Good job," I said.

"Thank you very much," he said. "I barely know how to play this game and there I go winning all this *money*. Sheesh."

Seth had quieted down, but I could see him simmering with anger. I had also been waiting for McCauley to reveal his hidden agenda. He probably keeps stacks of them under his bed.

At last, he squinted at Seth. "Hey, I know you."

The teenager blanched and pulled away a couple inches away from the table. "No, I don't think so."

"Sure I do. You're Lenny Scofield's boy. I used to live down the block from your family in Torrance."

Seth shook his head. "You're thinking of someone else."

"No, I'm sure of it," said McCauley. "Your name is Kevin Scofield. I remember when you were just a little boy. You don't remember me?"

Seth had become a piece of statuary. Every muscle in his body had frozen. He'd stopped breathing. His lips were an angry little knot.

"Old man," he said, "you're losing your mind."

The dealer began the next hand, but McCauley ignored him. "Kevin," he said, "I hope you don't mind me asking ... but what are you doing gambling? You're not twenty-one yet."

"Yes, I am," he said.

"Well, let's see," said the priest, leaning back and tapping his finger on his teeth. "The last time I talked to your father, he was upset about how you failed seventh-grade math. And that was five years ago, because he was calling to check up on me after my heart surgery."

McCauley paused, his eyes searching the ceiling. He ticked off the years on his fingers. "So that makes you in twelfth grade right now."

"That's ridiculous," said Seth. "I have identification."

The dealer's ears had pricked up. "Did you say that he was underage?"

Suddenly McCauley blushed. "Well, no, I didn't say *that*, it's just that—"

"But you did say that he was underage, correct?"

"It's, it's … just … not my place," McCauley stammered. "I mean, it's just that, you know … I don't want to overstep my bounds here."

I admired the Jesuit's brilliance. He'd faked an attack of conscience. Now it was up to the dealer to act.

It happened very quickly. The dealer twisted around and caught the eye of a nearby pit boss, who swooped over in the blink of an eye. He looked like a bird-of-prey that had just spotted a mouse on the ground below.

The dealer whispered something in the man's ear. The pit boss looked at Seth. The teenager looked about half a minute away from tears, but he was putting on a brave front.

"Sorry, but there seems to be a problem with your age," said the pit boss. "Could I see your ID?"

I noticed that the other players at the table had slipped away. Not me—I was sticking it out. In fact, I'd have sold popcorn. This was going to be entertaining.

"I'm twenty-one," said Seth.

"Then let's see your identification," the pit boss replied.

Seth scowled as he reached into his wallet and produced his fake driver's license and handed it to the pit boss. I had procured that ID for him. Now I regretted not taking it away from him during our showdown up in Santa Ynez.

The boss inspected it. "This says you're twenty-one," he said.

"By my calculation, he's in twelfth grade."

"The two aren't exclusive," said the boss.

"That's a good point," said McCauley. "Look, I'm sorry for causing a fuss, I didn't want to get anybody in trouble—"

The pit boss silenced him. "We appreciate the concern. The dealer informed me that you lived on the same street."

"Yes," said McCauley.

He eyed the fake license. "What was the name of the street?"

I tensed. He was testing McCauley on his story. The pit boss was no fool. He knew that this scam could have as many tentacles as an octopus.

The old priest hemmed and hawed, then cleared his throat. "My memory isn't what it used to be," he said.

"Try to remember," said the boss.

Then McCauley suddenly snapped his fingers, and his face lit up. "Poinsettia. The street was Poinsettia."

The pit boss looked at the driver's license. I held my breath. His face remained impassive.

"You're right," he said. "Do you remember the number?"

"Of *his* house?"

"Yes."

"Why would I know that?"

The pit boss looked at him. "If his house was close to your own, the numbers are probably close too. Give me an estimate."

McCauley nodded. "Okay, okay. I used to live at thirteen eighty-eight, and his family lived was three doors down, so let's see. The addresses in Los Angeles skip every six numbers. That means he was eighteen less."

I watched McCauley count off on his fingers again and had to stifle a laugh. The man could've beaten a team of actuaries in a mental math competition.

"Was it thirteen seventy?" he said.

The boss' eyes glanced up. "That's correct."

My jaw dropped. That wasn't a lucky guess. McCauley had left nothing to chance. He'd memorized the information on Seth's fake driver's license.

Seth looked like he wanted to melt into the floor. "My license says that I'm twenty-one," he said. "You're covered, okay?"

The pit boss narrowed his eyes. That was the wrong thing to say. He wasn't going to be party to a cover-up. This man lived to bust cheaters, probably took them very personally—and Seth had just messed with his pride.

"Kevin," he said, "I'm going to ask you to come with me. Gather your chips."

Seth threw his hands into the air. "What the hell? I didn't do anything *wrong*."

Something in his tone of voice sounded very adolescent. The pit boss must've noticed it too, because a wicked grin grew out the side of his face like a tumor. He nodded to a pair of polo-shirted security guards, who quickly stood on either side of Seth's chair.

For the second time in a week, I was watching the little craphead get collared. It felt good. I was pretty sure what was going to happen to him too. In the back, they'd cross-check his identity with other casinos. That's when they'd find out about his little debacle in Santa Ynez last week. He'd be out on his ear.

As I watched him go, I knew that he wouldn't be bothering us again that night—unless he turned us in.

McCauley turned to me. "Gosh, I hope I didn't cause any trouble."

"I'm guessing you probably did."

"Geez Louise." He looked authentically flustered. "Oh well. I wonder if I can find him to apologize."

I watched him for a quick wink, an acknowledgement of the ruse we were playing, but it never came. Father McCauley was a pro.

By now, he and I were the only two players left at the table. The dealer said, "Hold on, boss says we need a new shoe."

He stepped away. The old priest glanced around. The pit bosses were looking the other way. Nobody was within earshot.

He lifted his glass of whiskey to his mouth and spoke in a low but urgent tone. "Get the kids out of here," he said. "Seth will turn all of us in if he can find a way to make half a penny from it."

"Okay," I said from inside my drink. I made sure that my eyes were looking the other way.

He kept talking. "I'm going to the big money tables. There will be a chair open to my left. Join me in exactly one hour. Watch my backpack. Watch it closely. The second it hits the floor, switch it with Michael's bag and leave. Got it?"

I didn't understand why, but there was a lot I didn't understand about the mathematician priest. The wise thing was to agree.

"Okay," I said.

"You gotta watch me. We're going down to the wire."

"I will."

The dealer returned. McCauley assumed his doddering act again. "I'm ready to keep playing, if you'll have me."

"Absolutely," said the dealer. He turned to me. "What about you? The kid was right, you've been on a roll."

It was a new shoe, and I had a crew of teenagers to round up. "No, I'm gonna take a break." I nodded at McCauley. "Good luck tonight, old man."

SIXTY

I bought a pack of cigarettes and walked outside the casino. It was now eleven at night. My pockets were full of ten thousand dollars in black chips. I wondered how the others had been doing.

Outside the casino doors, I lit a cigarette. That was for three reasons. One, I needed the nicotine to steady my nerves. Two, it helped my cover, by making me look like a junkie gambler, suffering under a quivering mass of addictions. Three, I needed to find Michael, who had been in constant motion. I figured he would pass here soon enough.

I waited, puffing, watching the crowd flowing past my feet, thinking about my gambling life. It was ending tonight. I'd have to get serious again about my acting career. That would involve doing more stagework, which I was scared to death of. Stage actors were all exaggerated movements and projecting voices; bit television actors like me were more natural.

Soon enough, I spotted Michael's head bobbing above the throng of incoming gamblers. He wasn't going to see me, so I dog-whistled.

His ears caught the sound, and soon his eyes spotted me on the bench. He ran over.

"Nice to see you finally," I said. "I got eight thousand dollars in my pocket that needs some loving transportation."

"I've been so busy, dude. Did you hear?"

He was brimming with teenage boy excitement. "No. What's going on?"

"Perry and Samuel both got warned off."

"Warned off?"

"Yeah, they're not barred, but the pit boss told them they couldn't play blackjack anymore. They were making too much."

I lifted an eyebrow. "How much was too much?"

"Like, six or seven thousand each."

I did the math in my head. They were the team's best players. The others had probably earned half as much. That put the take at about thirty-five thousand, plus my own, which was forty-five thousand. Helen would add to that.

"That makes about fifty grand," I said.

It sounded like a lot, but we were only about halfway to our goal. Michael fidgeted. I could tell he was upset. I would be too, if I were the last man on the totem pole, depending on tonight's run to pay my way through college.

"I've got some other stuff to tell you," I said.

I summarized the events—Helen's calling McCauley, Seth's revenge, McCauley's arrival, his brilliant manipulation, the high-stakes tables.

"Oh man," he said. "If Seth rats on us, he's gonna get destroyed. Seriously."

"I don't think he will," I replied. "But let's assume he does. I need you to go and round up the team. You guys are finished."

Michael's face plummeted to his shoes. "But—"

"This is McCauley's order."

"Oh. What about you?"

I smiled. "I'm meeting McCauley at the high-stakes tables in less than an hour."

Michael punched his hand. "Oh, snap. I want to *see* that."

I shook my head. "Now go round up the other kiddies and head back to the van."

He looked hesitant, so I grew stern. "Stay strong, Michael. We're going to reach the goal."

He buckled under, and we fist-pounded. As he stood up, I said, "And once you've gotten all our chips out of the casino, I'll be waiting right here for you."

"Why?"

I gave him my best mysterious smile. "We have one more thing to arrange."

SIXTY-ONE

Months earlier, during one of our long nighttime van rides, McCauley had told me about high-stakes blackjack tables. He'd said that, in Las Vegas, an average card-counter had a better chance of landing on the moon than of getting into those rooms. They were the haunt of celebrities, titans of industry, and whales who had flown over from Macau to play three hands of poker at half a million per.

At this casino, tucked into the rolling hills northeast of San Diego, the high-stakes tables were fortunately a bit more accessible to mortal men. All it usually took in California, he'd said, was a buy-in.

I kept telling myself that as I approached the velvet rope that separated the riffraff from the high-stakes tables. A guard who looked like he'd been stitched into his own suit stood alongside one of the stanchions. His hand rested on the post, as though he were ready to block anybody who so much as glanced his way.

"What's the buy-in?" I asked.

"Three thousand."

I whistled low, under my breath. That was a lot of money. "Can I work it off doing dishes in the back?"

"We know you've got it," he said.

I grinned. "Oh, you know how to flatter a girl. What's the minimum?"

"Two fifty."

That was a lot better than Vegas casinos, where some of the tables had minimum bets of twenty grand.

"I'm in," I said. "Will you accept a kiss on a cheek for a tip?"

I'd pushed it too far. He looked at me like I'd just slathered myself in pink cake frosting and tossed a handful of glitter into the air. "Do some pushups or something, man."

"I thought you were supposed to be friendly to high-roller guests."

"I've watched you all night. You're not a high roller. Just give me the money or get out."

I handed over thirty black chips from my bag. He unhooked the velvet rope and I stepped into the VIP area.

My eyes swept the room. Over at the roulette table, a rouged, bored blonde was texting alongside her sweaty husband. His wild, round eyes told me that he was addicted to risk. I guessed that he worked in high finance.

On the other side of the room, at the pai-gow table, a group of Chinese men were playing soberly—until one suddenly quintupled his bet. According to McCauley, that was a hallmark of Asian players.

Over at the craps table, three women wearing tight gold sequined skirts leaned over the railing. I averted my eyes. There was to be no distractions here. Too much was on the line.

In fact, looking around, I was probably the tensest

person here. After all, most of these bastards sewed throw pillows out of hundred-dollar bills. I was authentically poor.

To the right I spotted the blackjack table. It was separated from the other games, and it was bathed in a warm glow of light. I recognized that glow. It was the same type of atmosphere created on television sets.

Perfect for filming.

I swiveled my head. A quick scan yielded at least six different black domes in the ceiling, all undoubtedly trained on our table, since blackjack was the easiest to cheat at. That didn't worry me much. After all, I didn't know how to count cards. In fact, my grand plan here was miniscule. I was just going to bet the minimum and hope not to get wiped out. At a two-hundred-fifty dollar per hand, I had enough for twenty-eight losses. It could happen.

McCauley, on the other hand, did need to worry about the eyes-in-the-sky. For the last hour, he'd been doing double duty, both counting and sweeping. I imagined that the typical counters' rules—about steaming, about not tipping your hand, about staying under the radar—all flew out the window when you scaled the tree this high.

As I approached the table, I could see that whatever McCauley had done was working. There was a huge heap of black chips on the baize. It looked like the god of gambling had favored him this evening.

As I took the seat to his left, I saw that the old priest was deeply into his doddering old man character. I listened as he successfully pestered everyone at the table with his stream of consciousness.

"You know," he was saying, "I can't find a way to understand this, how I just keep winning ... last year I lost my shirt at the Bellagio, I had to borrow money just to get to the airport ... have you seen that movie about luck? My daughter loves it, says I'm the poster child for chaos theory, whatever that means ... gosh I wish I could remember the name of that film ... it's a miracle I remember my own name ... oh, is it my turn? Sorry..."

I saw the empty glass in his hand. A waitress came along wearing a miniskirt the size of a cocktail napkin and replaced it with another drink.

So he was on a full bender. I couldn't judge him. Inebriation helped McCauley to enter this alternate persona, to act like a man whose faculties had left him and who had entered the most incredible run of luck. This was how he deflected investigation.

While the dealer swept up the cards for the next hand, I placed all my chips on the felt, then sorted them into neat stacks. It was a pathetic haul compared with his dragon's hoard.

McCauley watched me drunkenly. "Little bit OCD, aren't you?" he slurred.

"I just like to know what I'm dealing with."

"What you're dealing with," he replied, "is something I've been waiting my whole life for. A night like this. Look." He scooped up a handful of chips. "I won four thousand in the last three hands. My wife is going to love me. We can finally buy an RV."

"That's amazing," I said.

"Here, I want you to have some." He dumped the chips onto my square. "Take them. Congratulations."

He was slurring. I shoved the chips towards him. "No, sir," I said, "they're yours."

The old priest shoved them back. "You take them. I don't want them."

I noticed the pit bosses watching us. "Jesus, old man,

you probably will want them when you shake it off tomorrow morning. Let's just play separate games."

I shoved the chips back at him. This time, McCauley didn't resist. He turned dejectedly back towards the table.

As the dealer tossed us cards, I understood the scheme. He'd forced me to show to the pit bosses that we weren't working in cahoots.

We played a hand. I lost two hundred and fifty dollars. McCauley won another thousand. It seemed that the old saying was true—old age and treachery do overcome youth and skill. I discreetly watched his body language, his head, his eye movements, and I couldn't see him counting. This man was a sorcerer.

We went on like that for fifteen more minutes. I lost five more hands. With each loss, I saw the pit bosses visibly lose interest in me.

Meanwhile, McCauley won four and lost one, raking in another four grand. As he was muttering something about the lottery, I noticed something that made my skin crawl.

It was the wolf-man.

SIXTY-TWO

Last time, he'd been nosing around the main floor. This time, he was skulking around the VIP section. The wolf-man was probably the equivalent of an enforcer on a hockey team, the tough guy who ignored positions and who roamed wherever he might be needed to pursue and destroy.

I started to feel nervous. My disguise—a simple cowboy hat pulled low over my eyes—wasn't exactly original.

"I bet they're wondering how to stop you, old man," I said loudly.

"No, young man, they want me to keep going." McCauley threw back the rest of his whiskey. I noticed the old man's knees slumped against the table. He was blinking slowly.

The old priest was about to pass out. This was an emergency. I needed to get his chips out of the casino before things went bad.

Then a telephone rang. It was coming from the phone on the wall. One of the pit bosses picked up. He turned his back to us. I could see his finger dragging along a tablet computer in the corner. I caught a glimpse of what seemed to be surveillance photos.

This wasn't good. McCauley must've spotted the call too, because his jabbering suddenly took on a different tone.

"Jesus, look at all these chips," he said, slurring heavily now. "Clogging up the table. When it rains it pours. Best laid plans, mice and men. Pardon me friends. Pardon me."

He unhooked his backpack, which had been slung around the back of his chair, and began stuffing the chips inside, handful by handful. It took a long time. Casinos have designed tables so that players can't easily swipe the chips off.

On his final handful, McCauley dropped a few chips on the floor. It looked like an honest accident. When the old priest bent over to pick them up, however, he lost his balance. His head crashed into the side of the blackjack table, and he collapsed onto the floor at my feet.

"Jesus," I said.

I leaped off my chair. I'd been ignoring his antics, playing my hand, acting annoyed. However, at this point a fellow stranger might be honestly concerned, so my reaction was appropriate. My one question was whether he'd gone too far with the drunken gambler act, whether he was really and truly hammered.

One look at the reddened web of capillaries in his eyeballs told me it was the latter. I crouched next to him and hooked my hands under his armpits and lifted him back up onto his chair.

Then McCauley's eyes opened. For one moment, he looked at me with perfect clarity. It felt like when an old person gets that moment shortly before death. He didn't say anything. He didn't have to. The message in his eyes was unmistakable.

Now.

A thrill raced through my body. This was performance art at its highest form. I turned to the dealer. "You take care of this guy," I said. "I can't play here anymore. This section is too rich for my blood."

I swiped my remaining chips off the table and stuffed them into my pockets. Then I reached down.

The two identical Jansport backpacks were side-by-side at our feet. One was stuffed with black chips, glittering in the lighting. The other was empty. The actor in me was conscious that all this was being recorded from various angles. I could only hope to make the swap and to move swiftly.

As the security guard arrived and propped up the drunken priest, I lifted the bag with the black chips and quickly zipped it shut. Then I walked away from the table towards the red velvet rope.

The bouncer stood with his hand on the stanchion and gazed unsympathetically at me.

"Better luck next time, sweetheart," he said.

"Shut up and let me out."

I could see him looking for instructions from the pit bosses. My armpits were blooming with sweat. Evidently the bosses weren't giving any signals, because he slowly unhooked the red velvet rope and stepped aside.

I moved quickly past him, out of the high-stakes area, into the blackjack floor, past all the regular tables, then up the short set of stairs. Pausing at the top, I looked back.

The wolf-man was threading his way through the crowd towards me. His eyes connected with mine. He smiled viciously, revealing a row of sharp teeth.

Crap. The pit bosses had been watching all along. Maybe they'd already made a positive ID from our last encounter a few months earlier. The only advantage I'd really been given was McCauley's injury. That had distracted them enough to give me a minute's head start on them. I might not have even escaped out of the VIP area if it hadn't been for him.

I gulped. There was probably fifty thousand dollars' worth of chips in my backpack, and I needed to get it out of the casino.

Thank God I had a plan.

I turned tail and dove into the maze of slot machines. There were at least five hundred here, intentionally arranged in a haphazard way, so that gamblers lost their way. I hoped to use that against him.

A minute later, I glanced back. The wolf-man wasn't anywhere in sight, but he could be crouching around the next turn.

It was now or never. I wended my way out of the slots over towards the men's bathroom, which was near the main staircase. That meant crossing the open lobby. There would be no cover there.

I pulled my cowboy hat as low as possible over my eyes and walked into the lobby, trying to blend into the crowd. That meant slowing down my pace. It was the longest thirty meters of my life. As I approached the bathroom entrance, I glanced back.

The wolf-man was nowhere to be found. I exhaled. The last link in the chain was about to be snapped into place.

I turned and headed around the S-shaped entrance to the bathroom, walked all the way down the line of sinks. I pulled the backpack off my shoulder and slung it against the bottom of the last stall.

Then I turned to the sink and turned on the water. I held my hands under the automatic soap dispenser until the foam squirted out. Then I began scrubbing. It was the most thorough handwashing I'd ever done. A first-year surgical resident didn't scrub this well.

During that time, I kept my eyes fixed on the backpack in the mirror. I wondered what was taking so long.

Suddenly the backpack was yanked into the stall, like a piglet being grabbed by an invisible monster. A half-second later, the backpack was shoved out.

Empty.

I smiled to myself. Without bothering to dry my hands, I turned, picked up the empty bag, and left the bathroom.

In the massive lobby, I turned right. The sliding glass doors that were leading to the outside were right there, twenty seconds away. I began counting. Nineteen, eighteen, seventeen...

I was five strides away from the automatic mat when the figures stepped in front of me. I stumbled back, blinking. I was looking at two security guards in polo shirts.

"Sir," said one, "before you leave, we'd like to talk to you."

To the right, I saw the wolf-man sucking on his tooth. He was practically rubbing his hands together. "You sure you have the right person?" I said.

"We do," said one.

"I just lost a bunch of money in the VIP area," I said.

"We know," he replied. "Bring your bag."

I feigned disappointment. In the corner of my eye, I noticed Michael exiting the bathroom. He was casually carrying a soft yellow Jansport bag slung across one shoulder. He kept it on the opposite side of his body from me. I was glad that he'd been astute enough to buy one in a new color.

Michael casually joined the back of a group of high-spirited middle-aged women and began laughing as though at one of their jokes. He even made a charming comment, startling the women who laughed with surprised. He looked like a dutiful son out with his mother's friends at the casino.

It was the perfect cover. The good boy. The security guards watched him pass. They looked over at the wolf-man, who gave a tiny shake of the head.

I tried not to watch as Michael walked out the door and disappeared around the corner of the building. I dropped my head and gave silent thanks.

"All right, I'll come," I said to the security staff, "but I don't know what for."

SIXTY-THREE

For the next two hours, I was grilled like a piece of sausage.

Usually when a counter gets backed off, it's short and sweet. The pit boss announces, right there on the gambling floor, that the person is suspected of card-counting, and that further gambling is prohibited. The counter is escorted off the premises, maybe warned about further trespassing.

But not me. First they'd removed my hat and glasses. Then the wolf-man and two others questioned me for two hours. I summoned all my imaginative thespian powers and pretended that I was back in an improv class, assigned to play a downed American fighter pilot in a Soviet inter-rogation.

Who is the old man?

I don't know.

Who was Kevin?

I don't know.

Where are the women this time?

I don't know.

In fact, I only lifted my head once—at the moment they

opened my backpack. I wanted to see the looks on their faces. It was priceless.

I couldn't blame them for the roughing up. They had a good sense of suspicion, and we'd taken them for a lot of money that night. Not whale money, we were well below that level, but enough to put a good dent in the casino's monthlies.

I found myself thinking about McCauley, wondering if he was all right. I wanted to ask where he was, if he'd had any serious injuries, but that wouldn't be possible as long as I was in character. I consoled myself with the fact that an unconscious man generally didn't tell any secrets.

When they finally let me go, I had been photographed and formally barred. They'd informed me that they would be sharing the information with every other casino in the state. They also kept my bag as evidence.

All that was fine. I was finished with gambling anyways.

At two o'clock in the morning, the security guards finally escorted me out of the casino and down the driveway. At the large water fountain, they stopped walking, assumed a wide-legged stance, and crossed their arms.

"No goodbye kiss?" I said.

The wolf-man smirked. "Don't come back."

I began walking away and played it sad. I kicked a stone, carried my head low. There was no real reason for it except my actor's pride. The jig was up, I'd been banned, and they knew deep down that they'd just been had.

In the big scheme, I'd won.

Fifteen minutes later, I arrived at the parking spot where the van had been earlier that night.

It was gone.

I felt the anger rising. I should have known something

like this would happen. A double-cross. They weren't going to let me even collect my final commission. I pulled out my phone and called Helen. If she had truly cheated me, she wouldn't pick up, but it was worth the shot.

To my surprise, she answered on the first ring. "We got it," she said.

"How much?"

"The one hundred thousand dollars. We even got three thousand fifty extra."

"But what about McCauley?"

She paused. "We haven't heard anything. I guess we'll find out soon enough."

I felt something catch in my throat. "Okay. Well, guess I'll catch a bus home in the morning."

"Are you kidding?" she said. "We wouldn't desert our hero. We were waiting for you until fifteen minutes ago, but the boys got hungry so we had to hit In-N-Out."

"Oh," I said.

"By the way, Michael told us everything. Nice work, Jake. Don't move, we'll be right there."

I smiled and ended the call. Those were nice words, but as I stood on the street corner, watching passing traffic, I began thinking the big thoughts. About rising inequality, about the purpose of education, about Robin Hood characters becoming folk heroes in a time of declining middle class. About how elastic human morality could be. About Jesuit priests who acted like anything but.

And mostly about what I had to return to. An empty apartment, an acting career in critical condition, a selfish life. In fact, this team had taught me a valuable lesson—that it felt *good* to live for someone else.

The van pulled up in front of me, and I stowed away

those thoughts. As the door opened, I felt hands pulling me inside. The sounds of cheering filled my ears.

The team.

SIXTY-FOUR

I didn't hear anything more for almost two weeks after that. The sun continued to rise and set, animal species continued to go extinct in the rainforest, the surf continued to be flat and inconsistent. I was a bug crawling on the enormous windshield of life. It was up to other people to change the world.

Then, while strolling on the beach one afternoon, feeling the skin on my cheeks start to crackle in the dry winter wind, I heard my phone beep. I pulled it from my pocket. It was a text from Michael. He wanted some help with an English assignment.

There wasn't any reason to say no, and I needed the money, as usual. I replied in the affirmative.

At seven o'clock the next night, I turned onto his street, parked, and headed up his dingy front walk. The wildebeest's door was still festooned with paper flyers from take-out restaurants.

I climbed the stairs and knocked. Michael answered immediately, and I stepped inside.

We sat down at the kitchen table and looked at each other. It was awkward being back in this simple kitchen.

"I had my interview with a Georgetown alumnus yesterday," he finally said.

"And?"

"It was good. We talked for almost an hour."

"That's a long time."

"Yeah, he cancelled his next appointment so I could tell him about card-counting."

"The team is public knowledge now?"

"Sure," he said. "It's finished, right? We might as well brag that we were the last graduating class of Patrick McCauley's School of Gambling."

"Songs will be sung," I said. "Have you heard anything about him?"

Michael looked sad. "He's gone from school. They said he's at Manresa for good. Father James said something about wearing a bib and being spoon-fed. Did he fall or something?"

I nodded somberly. So that final fall on the carpet hadn't been faked. He'd really injured himself. It'd been a final sacrifice, of sorts, for the card-counting team, his *raison d'être*.

This was depressing me. McCauley had been a larger-than-life presence, the type of person about whom stories are told for decades after death. I felt something wet welling up in my eyes and changed the subject.

"So where's this English assignment?" I said.

Michael grinned. "There isn't one," he replied. "I needed to lure you over here somehow."

My heart stopped. This was feeling too familiar, and I'd already learned that I didn't like the taste of entrapment.

He read the look on my face. "Settle down. Helen just wanted me to give you something."

He reached into his book bag and tossed a vinyl pencil case on the table. I scowled. "She obviously didn't get the memo. I only accept Hello Kitty pencil cases."

"Open it," he said.

Shrugging, I unzipped the case and dumped it upside down. A stream of black chips poured out and clattered onto the table. They carried the smell of the casinos— alcohol, stale cigarette smoke, desperation. It already felt unfamiliar, like a dream that could barely be remembered.

"All for me?" I said.

Michael nodded. "She said it's your last commission. She said it was four thousand. You can count it, if you want. Here's a note for verification."

I read her note, then crumpled it up. I didn't need to count the chips. I knew that Michael hadn't cheated me. I immediately began to hatch a plan that involved driving to Temecula with a friend, who would return the tokens. The only name that kept coming to mind was Brody, the scuzzball. I didn't have many other friends.

"You could've kept this."

He grew uncomfortable. "Hey, we couldn't have done it without a sweeper like you. I mean, you're personally sending me to college."

So I *had* made a difference, in at least one life. Still, I don't like sentimentality, so I played it off, shrugging. "It's not like I had a choice, you asshole."

He laughed. I collected the chips and put them in the bag. Then we both stood up from the table at the same time. At the door, I stopped and turned.

"Keep in touch, man. Let me know when you get your acceptances."

"I will."

I shut the door behind me. At the bottom of the stairs, I took a black chip and crouched down and slid it under the wildebeest's door. I knocked on the wood and then walked away.

It was more than she deserved, but I'm a man of my word.

PLOTWORKS PUBLISHING

If you enjoyed this story, please leave a review at the place where you purchased it.

Then visit Plotworks Publishing to follow Jake Logan on his next *noir* mystery!

Now turn the page for a sneak peek—

She's his worst
nightmare.
HYSTERICAL
FOR HARVARD
A JAKE LOGAN
PRIVATE TUTOR
MYSTERY
J.A. JERNAY

HYSTERICAL FOR HARVARD

Acting is probably the most unstable profession in the world, and somewhere around my twenty-eighth birthday, I realized that my luck had finally run out.

After almost a decade of steady work that paid the bills, I hadn't gotten a part in six months. I hadn't even gotten an audition in three. So the result was inevitable.

I'd become a waiter.

My new workplace was the Earthen Jug, an unbearably trendy patio café in Santa Monica. Most of my time was spent slinging low-carb Asian lettuce wraps to girls wearing too many accessories and not enough underwear.

So far, I'd learned that food service really wasn't for me. Handling meals all day leaves a weird stench on your finger-tips. It smells like nothing else in the world, and won't wash off either. I'd also learned that the squishiness of the food bothered me too. I found myself dreaming of firm substances, things that wouldn't rot, sour, or jiggle.

Still, I'm glad that I started working there, because the restaurant was where Jarvis found me—and that's where my life changed.

I was turning a corner, balancing a plate of *huevos rancheros* in each hand, when I spotted him in my section, one leg crossed over the other, intently reading a copy of the Chronicle of Higher Education. He looked as relaxed as a grandfather on a porch during a summer rain.

But if there's one thing I remembered about Jarvis, it's that there no such thing as a coincidence when he's around. He was here for a reason—and it was probably me.

I walked up to him hesitantly.

"The eagle flies at morning light," I said.

"With the might of a thousand armies," he replied. His eyes flicked up briefly. He was smiling.

It was the code to the Owl and Pigeons, our secret society at Harvard.

I have two major secrets in my life, and now you know the first one. I went to Harvard University.

I never really talk about it. People really look at you differently. We call it dropping the H-bomb. Sometimes people think that every person who goes there is loaded with money. That's not even remotely true. Lots of ordinary kids are swimming eyeball-deep in the two hundred thousand dollars in loans that they take out to afford the degree. Those are the middle-class kids. The really poor ones have the best deal. If your parents together earn less than fifty grand a year, Harvard doesn't make you pay a cent.

Jarvis had been one of those poor kids.

He'd told me that he was from Detroit. His father had been a spot welder on the auto assembly lines until he got laid off, and then he didn't work for ten years. Jarvis had told me about his family the first time either of us had ever gotten drunk, in his dorm room on a Friday night. I remember that he'd been so poor in college that he couldn't even afford textbooks. He'd borrow a classmate's books, read the next two weeks' of assignments in a single night, scribbling notes.

Sometimes Jarvis would host poker nights for wealthy freshmen. He'd get them drunk, then beat their pants off at the card table. I remember people losing hundreds of dollars to him. Beating Harvard undergraduates at games of strategy isn't any small peanuts either, as you can imagine. Still, everybody knew that he needed the money, so nobody ever begrudged him the winnings.

In short, he was the kind of guy whom everybody knew was going somewhere.

I wasn't very wealthy either. Some of the other Harvard students had smeared our faces in it. The ones you'd think were smart enough to laugh at all that elitist crap are the ones who embraced it the most. Yapping in their ridiculous lockjaw Boston accent, they'd denied us entrance to all the best parties. We weren't invited into any of the secret fraternities.

So Jarvis and I had decided to invent our own secret society. We'd named it the Owl and Pigeons. We had our first meeting in the basement of an off-campus Italian restaurant and drunk dry sherry boosted from the kitchen. We'd posted fake flyers announcing a dress-up day for anybody who wanted into our group. Nobody had really responded. It'd been a fun but pitiful little way of imitating the rich boys.

And so here we were, ten years later, still using our secret code.

I said earlier that I had two secrets. If you're waiting for the second one, you're going to have to wait a while longer. I'm not going to tell you that one yet.

Jarvis lifted his face from the publication. Up close, he looked exactly the same as he had in college. He had shiny cheeks, as though he moisturized with canola oil. Every hair was in its place. He wore a smart gray suit with a black tie. He always looked as if he were about to step onstage.

"How's the breakfast burrito?" he said.

"Today, good," I said. "Yesterday, not so good."

"New recipe?"

"New cook."

"It feels like a long time since college," he said. "Doesn't it?"

"I guess," I said.

His eyes traveled over my sauce-splattered smock. I felt embarrassed. Our old friends were becoming scholars, senators, surgeons. I was on my way to becoming assistant weekend manager.

I tipped my chin up and went on the offensive. "So tell me ... how are *you* earning your daily bread these days?"

"Education," he said.

"Really? I'd always thought you'd be a spook."

"A spook?" He looked perplexed. "You mean a spy?"

"Yeah."

Jarvis laughed. "Are you kidding? Spook hours are *terrible*."

"But you always loved surveillance. Remember Heather Brighton's closet?"

"You bet," he said, smiling at the memory. "Sorry, no government work for me. Too many rules and regulations."

Suddenly I felt impatient with this impromptu encounter with my past. I wanted to get out of it. "What can I get you for lunch?"

"I have a job opportunity for you," he said. "Where can we talk?"

He looked at me intently, gauging my reaction. Then the tiniest crinkle of amusement appeared at the corner of his mouth. Jarvis knew that I couldn't refuse, not *here*, when he'd seen my day job.

"I'm not off my shift until three," I said.

"Then come into the office tomorrow." He handed me his business card. It said *Kenneth Jarvis, M.S.W., Ph.D. Academic Consultant.*

"What exactly is an academic consultant?" I asked.

"I help high school students get into college."

"Don't they have counselors to do that?"

He shrugged. "Most high school counselors don't have enough time. Or resources. Lots of them are getting canned." He spread his arms wide. "I'm here to fill the gap."

I balanced the card in my hand, feeling its heft, toying with the idea. I'd learned long ago that when Jarvis had an idea, it was a good idea to follow him, because it usually worked out.

"I don't know."

"Come in at nine," he said. "You know you want to."

I must've looked hesitant, because he urged me even harder. "Do it for the O and P."

He stuck out his fist. Our old signature goodbye. I couldn't resist. My fist pounded his in the stupid pattern we'd invented—up, down, twice left, twice right, then three finger snaps. I hate to say it, but it felt good to have been part of that stupid made-up fraternity.

"All right," I said.

He smiled. "You're making the right decision, Jake."

"Speaking of decisions, have you decided what you want?"

"What's good here?"

"I told you the breakfast burrito was okay."

"Can you bring me a menu?"

"Sure."

As I went off in search of a menu, he lifted his coffee mug to his lips and went back to his newspaper. When I returned, the mug and the paper had been laid on the table —but Jarvis was gone.

PLOTWORKS PUBLISHING

Visit Plotworks Publishing to explore a new series by J.A. Jernay—the Cosmo Bennett Mapping Thrillers!
Turn the page for another sneak peek—

J.A. JERNAY

BOUNDARY

A COSMO BENNETT MAPPING THRILLER

FROM THE AUTHOR OF THE AINSLEY WALKER
GEMSTONE TRAVEL MYSTERY SERIES

BOUNDARY

Cosmo and his assistant Noah shuffled down the dirt shoulder of the boulevard in the midday heat, sweating and miserable.

Each was lost in his own thoughts. Cosmo dreamed of hitting a heavy punching bag at his gymnasium. Noah dreamed of passing level nineteen of Operation Earlobe, an obscure RPG he'd abandoned last semester.

The morning's meeting had been a complete bust.

"I don't think we should continue," said Cosmo finally.

Noah didn't respond, but Cosmo took no notice. He continued: "I don't think anybody here takes our task seriously. I don't think this propaganda map was as influential as they say. I don't think this map has driven the civil unrest. I think social media and centuries of tribal warfare are more to blame for the unrest than anything else."

He looked over at Noah, waiting for a response. "What about you?"

The graduate assistant came back from his reverie. "Huh?"

"Did you hear anything I said?"

"No."

"I was just saying this is pointless and we should go home."

"I don't have a problem with that."

They arrived at Vida e Caffe. It was a chain café, with hundreds of similar franchises scattered across the southern half of the African continent. The branding was modern and inviting. A hundred people sat beneath umbrellas at small tables on the large outdoor patio.

An arm was waving at them. It was Christopher, their fixer, a cup of tea on a ceramic saucer in front of him. Two other cups awaited them.

"Hello sirs," he said. "I ordered us all a rooibos. It's a vanilla tea that is extraordinary."

Cosmo and Noah pulled out the chairs and sat down. The driver quickly sussed out that something was wrong.

"It was a bad meeting?" he said quietly.

"Yes," said Cosmo, "there was no progress made."

"I'm very sorry."

Cosmo sighed. "I think we have to leave."

The fixer looked confused. "But you just sat down—"

"The country," he clarified. "We have to leave Faba-jouti. We can't seem to do any good here."

Christopher looked crestfallen. "I do understand your frustration."

Noah said, "If it's okay with you, we'd probably like to just get in the car and go back to the hotel."

The fixer rediscovered his manners. "Of course, as you wish—"

"But we'd love to try the tea first—" added Cosmo.

"You two enjoy the rooibos," said Christopher, "while I fetch the car. The parking lot is very jammed and it will take quite a while to remove. I've already paid the bill."

Before they could object, the driver had shot to his feet. He clapped Cosmo on the shoulder and left the patio. They watched him cross the boulevard to an off-street parking area that was crammed tightly with vehicles. On his approach, the attendant began shifting other vehicles.

Noah sipped the tea. "This does taste really good. I don't drink enough tea."

"I like tea," said Cosmo. He sipped from the cup. "This one is good."

"What's your favorite?" asked Noah.

"Maybe pu'er."

"That one's bitter, right?"

"Yeah. It's fermented."

"What about Earl Grey?"

"A cliché."

"I think I'm more of a fruity tea guy," said Noah.

Cosmo nodded. "Yeah, they have their charms."

"You ever try chamomile?"

"It's good for sleeping," said Cosmo, "but otherwise it's—"

His comment was cut short by a massive fireball that erupted from the parking lot across the street.

———

In a split second, Cosmo and Noah instinctively rolled off their chairs and onto the ground beneath their table. Their eyes met. Each was filled with terror.

Then the shock of the overpressure hit. Cosmo felt the force of the blast wave hit the left side of his body. The highly compressed air rattled the left side of his skull. It even sent his lips and cheeks flapping to the right.

The initial sound of the explosion was deafening, but

that was soon replaced by a symphony of falling destruction. A thousand pieces of metal, plastic, glass, and upholstery rained down upon the boulevard, the grass, the other cars.

A shower of tiny shrapnel hit on the patio of the cafe. One hit Noah in the hand and sizzled his flesh. He shook it off.

They waited another few seconds for the shrapnel rain to end. Then Cosmo and Noah lifted their heads.

The patio of the café was transformed into pandemonium. The patrons started to pull themselves up from the ground and flee out to the street and in the opposite direction. The street itself was coming alive with panicked people running in every direction.

"What the actual—" said Noah.

"Christopher!" interrupted Cosmo. "What about Christopher?"

He scrambled up to his feet. Without waiting for Noah, he sprinted out of the café and across the boulevard, weaving through the stopped cars. The air was acrid with chemicals and the heat had somehow intensified even further.

The parking lot was a field of wreckage. The bomb had exploded in the middle of the space, shredding every vehicle and person within twenty meters. Pieces of concrete and metal and glass had been blown across the scene.

"Christopher!" he shouted again. "Christopher! Don't do this!"

He saw a shoe with a foot still in it. He saw a red string of guts entangled in a hubcap. A wave of nausea gripped his stomach. He covered his nose with his t-shirt and backed away.

He tripped backwards over a piece of metal, stumbled, and fell to the ground.

That's when he saw it.

A long strip of shredded fabric. A yellow-and-green printed tropical shirt.

It was bloody and torn.

Cosmo turned his head and retched onto the asphalt. All the tea he'd just drank came out.

He somehow pulled himself to his feet and staggered back to the café. Noah was waiting at the far corner, on the sidewalk, pacing frantically.

"So?"

"I found him," said Cosmo. He forced the next words out. "A little bit."

Noah's face went white. "Oh my God."

Cosmo didn't say anything. He just gripped Noah by the upper arm. "Walk with me. And don't look back."

The pair moved briskly down the boulevard, away from the scene. People were running past them, mouths open, eyes full of fear, but Cosmo maintained a steady pace. His face betrayed an intense desire to appear as normal as possible.

"So we're just going to leave the scene?" said Noah.

"Yep."

"Why?"

"Don't make me answer that, Noah."

"I think we should talk to the police, cooperate, tell them everything—"

"In a different country," Cosmo replied, "in a different scenario, you'd be right. But not here, not now."

Noah looked back over his shoulder at the scene.

"Look straight ahead," Cosmo said through his teeth, "and listen to me. Our Mercedes is gone. Christopher is ... gone."

"Shit—"

"And I'm going to suggest something else that could blow your mind."

"What?"

"It's possible that we were the intended target."

"That's insane."

"Is it?"

"How do you know?"

"I don't. But it's a possibility. Here's another one. It's possible that we are going to be used as scapegoats. We were the last people seen eating with Christopher. Do you want to be put in a Fabajouti jail on suspicion of a crime?"

They walked for another half minute in silence. Behind them, the chaos grew distant.

"Where are we going?" Noah said finally.

"Back to the hotel."

"And then?"

"We're leaving, like we planned."

"We're not going home, are we?" said Noah.

Cosmo's mouth grew hard and his jaw jutted out. He stared straight forward at an invisible point on the horizon. "No, we're not."

PLOTWORKS PUBLISHING

And be sure to explore J.A. Jernay's best-known series—the Ainsley Walker Gemstone Travel Mysteries!

Turn the page for a final sneak peek—

THE

URUGUAY AMETHYST

AN AINSLEY WALKER
GEMSTONE TRAVEL MYSTERY

J.A. JERNAY

THE URUGUAY AMETHYST

Ainsley pulled the backseat door closed. Her driver's eyes looked at her in the rearview mirror.

"Where can I take you?" Oswaldo asked in Spanish.

"Back to Tabarez," she said.

He nodded, and they pulled away from the curb. Ainsley studied him in the mirror. His jaw was set firmly. She decided to see what she could learn from him.

"Do you like working for Tabarez?" she said.

"Yes," he said. Nothing else.

Of course he wouldn't comment on his employer. She decided to stick to facts.

"Oswaldo, after lunch I will need you to help me take a very large package to this address." She handed him the paper with Bernabé's address. "Can you find this place?"

He read the address and nodded. Not a word. Ainsley was beginning to wonder if he was a bit simple.

The car was slicing down La Rambla, and Ainsley contented herself with staring out the window, at the blurring breakwall and at the choppy brown water of the delta.

The sky was bright blue and the clouds puffy and white and a chill wind was blowing again.

It was mesmerizing. She wrapped her coat around herself more tightly and snuggled in.

Then she woke up to Oswaldo touching her knee. The vehicle had stopped. She was outside Tabarez's house.

Ainsley emerged from the vehicle and buttoned the top collar of her coat. "It's so cold here," she said.

Oswaldo didn't respond. Conversationally, there was no difference between her driver and a piece of drywall. She decided to just issue him orders instead. It would save both of them a lot of trouble.

"Stay here until I return."

He lit a cigarette and looked straight ahead.

Slinging her purse over her shoulder, Ainsley walked alone towards the house. Her stomach was twisting itself into anxious knots. Partly because of El Árbol Negro, partly because she was so hungry.

And nervous. She was about to enjoy homemade *ñoquis* in a private dining room with an extremely wealthy and attractive man who may or may not have refused to sleep with her, even after she'd thrown herself at him. Why did she have to black out on *that* night of *all* nights? And now he was going to sell her a famous amethyst after telling her its secret history.

This felt too good to be true.

The copper gate was rolled wide open. Ainsley cocked her head. That was strange, given the value of the contents inside the mansion.

She stepped through the open gate onto the driveway, then moved into the manicured yard. It made her heart sing again. She touched the bougainvillea, listened to the branches clacking in the breeze from the estuary.

Then she rang the front doorbell and waited. The slab of wood before her was exquisite. Spirals and whorls had been dug into its surface, like the enormous thumbprint of a criminal.

There was no response. That was weird. Heinrik was the epitome of the efficient manservant. He should've been there in a flash.

She rang the doorbell again, then turned and surveyed the landscaping. Water was trickling from some unseen fountain. She couldn't find it. An invisible bird sang crookedly from the branches of a tall ash. She couldn't find that either. A sinking feeling filled her stomach.

Had she been lied to? Had Tabarez cast her aside that quickly? Had he decided to keep El Árbol Negro? She'd heard the old cliché of how Latin people lived for the moment, but this expulsion was quicker than she'd expected. She felt anger sprouting from her back like a bouquet of hot orange flames.

Upset, she turned back to the door. If he wouldn't answer the door, she would invite herself inside. She gripped the doorknob and turned it. The slab of wood swung open easily, as though it weighed ten pounds instead of twenty times that much. Of course Tabarez had made sure that the hinges were well-oiled.

She entered the foyer and noticed a large object, wrapped in black plastic, resting immediately next to the door.

El Árbol Negro.

With her fingertips she traced its lovely branches beneath the plastic. So beautiful. She noticed a dolly sitting next to it. How thoughtful.

Remembering her host's orders, she kicked off her shoes,

then crept around the edges of the carpet. The house was completely silent.

"José Ignacio?" she shouted. "Heinrik?"

Still no response. She crept up the stairs to the second floor sitting room where she had last seen him, in his white robe, strumming his instrument.

As she rose to the landing, she caught her breath.

José Ignacio was still sitting on the sofa in the sumptuous second floor *sala*. The guitar was laying next to him. His head was tilted back, and his eyes were shut. A thin smile decorated his mouth.

Another thin smile, this one quite a bit redder, and eight inches across, decorated his throat.

José Ignacio Tabarez was not going to be dining with her this afternoon.

He was dead.

PLOTWORKS PUBLISHING

Visit Plotworks Publishing today for all these titles—and
more!